THE OTHER SIDE OF THE LAW

KATELYNN RENTERIA

outskirts
press

Outskirts Press, Inc.
http://www.outskirtspress.com

Paperback ISBN: 978-1-4787-9099-0

Library of Congress Control Number: 2017910722

Cover Photo © 2017 thinkstockphotos.com. All rights reserved - used with permission.

Outskirts Press and the "OP" logo are trademarks belonging to Outskirts Press, Inc.

PRINTED IN THE UNITED STATES OF AMERICA

Prologue

ike a rain drop on velvet, I silently dropped from a dusty airshaft to the floor of Spades Enterprises, clad in navy and shrouded in the dark.

I glanced around the Tech Lab I had landed in, knowing that a door was 32 ft. to my left, thanks to the building blueprints I had memorized 16 hours earlier.

Almost subconsciously, I began to carry out my mission, silently gliding across to the floor to the main computer at the back of the computer lab.

I unclipped a mini-flashlight from my utility belt, shone it on the desktop, and switched on the PC.

While the computer warmed up, I slipped a USB Drive out of my pocket and held it millimeters away from the port I was going to plug it into.

I counted down how much time I had before the left-wing security guard came into the lab for a routine check.

64 seconds.

Plenty of time.

The second the computer's lock screen came up, I plugged in the USB Drive.

I watched expectantly as the screen went from displaying Spade Enterprises' logo to an array of speeding numbers on a green background.

I smiled as the algorithm on the drive unlocked the computer and pilfered through the files, picking out any of particular interest.

While the USB Drive was working its magic, I began to search the drawers for any folders or documents that would provide any vital information.

Oddly, the drawers were filled with pens, paper clips, calculators, and other generic office supplies.

Yet, there were no folders or documents in sight.

I carefully stripped a paper off of a sticky notes pad, folded it, and slipped it into my pocket, as a souvenir.

My internal clock told me that 38 seconds remained before the guard came in, and as if on cue, the computer screen flashed brightly.

The USB Drive had done its job, and I knew that it had copied files and erased any potential digital fingerprints of mine with efficiency.

With 22 seconds left, I had unplugged the USB, turned off the computer and made my way to the airshaft I had popped out from.

I unclipped a rope and hook from my belt, and I threw it up to the shaft.

The hook sailed through the opening, attached to the frame, and I began to pull myself up.

Once I was safely in the shaft, I rolled up my rope and hook and clipped it back onto my belt.

No sooner had I placed the cover of the shaft back onto the opening, the guard opened the door and stepped into the room.

Mission accomplished.

Chapter One

*J*t doesn't take a genius to know that often there is more than meets the eye. Every book has a story behind its unique cover. All facial expressions have a hidden thought buried beneath. Nothing is exactly what it seems, except for the things that are. It takes a skilled eye to tell the difference between the two.

My school is the type of facility that seems like your average run-of-the-mill joint middle/high school, yet it is so much more. At my school, students are trained to be able to look behind the cover and really see what lies underneath, even if it means putting on a cover of their own. What else would you expect from a school for spies? Or, at least, the part of the school that actually teaches spy-related things.

The thing about Henderson High is that it really and truly is a school, with kids ranging from 6th-12th grade learning your normal subjects like Algebra, Biology, World History, and Physical Education. But the thing that makes Henderson High special is its ability to hide in plain sight, with its *unique* students learning even *more* unique skills.

If you take advanced courses or AP classes like me, then you're in for subjects like Dialects and Calligraphy of the World (DCW), where 16 different languages are taught, learned and spoken. Covert Field Operations (CFO) is another one of my courses, where students learn the art of being a spy in the field (including all 856 different ways to spy on a person using a reflective surface).

The rest of the school learns the normal curriculum just like every other school in the nation. The only catch is, the "normal" students have absolutely no idea what goes on behind the closed doors of the advanced classes. It's the best part of hiding in plain sight. Spy kids at Henderson get the best of both worlds, without the hefty paperwork and fake I.D's (We get those senior year).

Most spy kids at Henderson are aiming for a career following the Field Course (FC), where some serious butt-kicking and world-saving goes down on a daily basis - but working in the field isn't the only option. There's also the Technical Operation Course (TOC) of study, where the more brainy of the spy breed learn to manipulate technology and work behind the scenes, the exact *opposite* of field agents.

However, there is an option that combines the two: the Covert Field Research Course (CFRC). This is what I'm currently taking; spies on this course of study learn how to hack *and* smack. We can manipulate any piece of technology handed over to us, from satellites to Blackberry phones. On top of that, we get the rush of hunting down bad guys in the field.

Life at Henderson can be stressful, especially with the surplus of assignments, projects, and extracurricular activities each student has to take care of. But there is one time a day where all that stress can just completely fade away in a few intense minutes: PE.

I remember one of our competitive days, when everyone took turns on a single indoor obstacle course to see who would take the #1 spot that week. Last week it was a tie between James Peters and I; the #1 spot usually fluctuated between us.

As soon as our coach started the timer, I hit the ground running as I twisted, vaulted, and cartwheeled through an intricate net of lasers. (Don't worry, these lasers were just normal lights. The *real* lasers come junior year.) Once I made it through the last one, I ran at full speed towards a metal wall that was timed to close in approximately 15.25 seconds.

My feet pounded on the pavement floor of our colossal gymnasium as I keyed in security codes on my Holographic Wrist

Manipulator Watch (HoloWatch). The metal door in front of me was about to close, and my shot at an A was growing thinner with every centimeter the door shut. I punched in a string of code, and the door stopped closing just long enough for me to slide under and make it across to the other side.

"Nice work Miss Verdant," my PE instructor, Mrs. Oslo, said, "Let's see if you can scale the wall."

I kept running as fast as I could towards a towering mountain of plastic rock, which I leapt onto and began to climb as fast as possible without taking a painful fall. Some of the hand and foot holds crumbled as I grabbed them, and I had to keep my reflexes on high alert to grab for a sturdy one. Once I made it to the top, I braced myself for what was coming.

"Mr. Cho, you're on!" Mrs. Oslo bellowed to the assistant coach. Not a second after she said that, a gust of wind stronger than all the fans in the school combined came at me, raging and wanting to ruin my chance at the top spot. I held my ground and tried as I hard as I could to maintain my balance. This test of endurance was always my least favorite of the bunch. I had to go against the wind and make it to a rope at the end of the wall, which I would then use to make my way down the fake mini-mountain and be one step closer to claiming my place as the victor.

I dropped down onto my knees and began crawling towards the rope. My limited body space caused the majority of the wind to slide right off of me, but the rest kept coming, and it showed no sign of letting up. My palms dug into the fake rocks as I tried to get a good grip and keep from flying away like a tumbleweed.

Eventually I made it to the rope, but not without a few close-calls and lots of hair in my face. "Come on, Kay, you got this!" My best friend Scarlet screamed from 55 feet below me.

Scarlet was about 2 inches taller than me, with long jet black hair and brown eyes. Her favorite color in the word was purple, and it was apparent in almost every article of clothing and object she owned. She was a good student who absolutely loved kicking butt in the field. There was no one I would rather have as my best friend.

I attempted a thumbs-up at her support but got a painful slap of wind on my hand instead, so I made a promise to myself to thank her afterwards.

A few more crawling steps, and I had finally made it to the rope. In six quick leaps down I was back on solid, non-windy ground.

For my final challenge, I had to pole vault over a very high bar onto a semi-soft mat.

What fun.

I plucked a pole from the pile and raced towards the bar.

I had to time my vault just right, and when I twisted to land on my back I had to be in the proper position.

Once I knew in my head that it was time to vault, I did it with grace and ease, twisting so that my back faced the mat and so I wouldn't hit the bar on the way down.

Once I hit the mat and jumped up on my feet, my run was over.

"TIME!" Coach Oslo yelled. "How long?" She asked Mr. Cho.

He glanced at the stopwatch in his hand from where he stood by the wind switch and announced, "5 minutes, 8 seconds."

"Yes!" I yelled, "That's a new record!"

"It certainly is Miss Verdant," Coach Oslo said proudly, "And the first go of the day, too. Well done."

I beamed as I walked over to the bleachers and gulped down my Orange Gatorade, tremendously proud of my accomplishment.

"Great job out there," James Peters told me as he passed by, "but don't get too comfortable. You're not the only one who has ever broken a course record." He grinned at me.

I smiled back. "I'll keep that in mind. Good luck." I replied.

James was a tall guy with dimples and wavy black hair. He had the slightest hint of arrogance in him, enough for it to be apparent though not too much to be annoying. Most of the time, anyway. He excelled in P.E and took pride in the skills he exhibited in the gym. He loved to show off.

"Thanks, but I don't think I'll need it." He called over his shoulder as he jogged to his place at the starting position.

I rolled my eyes and continued to drink my Gatorade. James really was a cool guy, but his ego was bound to get him into trouble someday. Everyone at Henderson knew that, even the 6th graders. But when the day comes that he *does* get into trouble because of it, we'll all be there for him. That's just the way we kids were at Henderson, spies or no spies.

I watched as James ran the course almost flawlessly (He almost fell face first into a particularly high laser), and in the end his time was 5 minutes, 10 seconds.

"No!" He shouted, kicking at the floor with his sneakers. "TWO seconds? Are you *kidding me?!*"

I smothered a laugh from my spot on the bleachers and continued enjoying my wonderful orange drink. As I took a breather, I watched the different grade levels and their different PE exercises.

The 8th graders were fencing each other in the left corner while defending a box that was behind them, trying to make it close enough to their opponent's box to snatch it.

The freshmen were practicing shooting crossbows in a boxed off area at the right corner of the gym, and I could tell from all of the arrows stuck in the unbreakable glass that some kids still needed a lot of practice.

James wandered over to the bleacher and took his usual spot at the very top. A little while after he sat down, Scarlet came over, bright faced and cheery.

"6 minutes even," she told me through heavy breaths, "That's good, right?"

"It's great," I replied, handing over her special PE towel, "And thanks for the encouragement, by the way."

Scarlet smiled. "What are best friends for?"

I grinned back.

Soon more kids who had run through the course claimed their own spot on the bleachers, and once everyone had run through, Coach Oslo walked with the final kid to the bleachers.

"Listen up Soaps!" She yelled (Soaps are what she called us sophomores). "Tomorrow we'll be starting a new unit, Unit 21:

Defensive Maneuvers in Motion. Ladies and gentlemen, tomorrow we play soccer!"

A couple of the boys cheered at her announcement, while some girls groaned in response.

"Oh, come on, it's not that bad. Just a friendly game of soccer, with some offensive slides, steals, and flying tackles thrown in here and there."

"Great..." One boy said sarcastically, "I can go home with cleat scars on my shin."

"Those are called 'battle scars' my friend. They're just a part of the job." Coach said in reply. She glanced at her watch, waited a few seconds, then blew her silver whistle.

"CLASS DISMISSED! CLEAN UP, AND HAVE A GREAT DAY!!!" She bellowed to everyone in the gym.

No sooner had she yelled that last word, everyone jumped up and scrambled to get ready for the incoming PE class. Obstacle courses were disabled, and the obstacles sunk underneath the floor. Helmets were stocked in high security cabinets hidden behind a secret hoax wall. Equipment was stuffed into their designated crates, and then hauled off into the gigantic chest with three separate locks held by three separate coaches and coach assistants.

All of this was done to make sure the "normal" students wouldn't accidentally stumble upon the laser grid and unravel the secrets of their gifted students.

Like I said earlier, Henderson spies get the best of both worlds.

While the coaches quadruple checked that the students didn't forget any security protocols (that would mean detention for the entire grade), the rest of us scampered off to the locker rooms to change and set off for our next classes.

I was already packing up the last of my things in my backpack when Suzy Lorenz bounded up to me.

"Sooo, Kay," Suzy drawled while snapping her gum, "You, like, totally kicked butt on the obstacle course today."

"Thanks Suzy," I replied, "I really tried today."

Suzy twirled a piece of her hair as she said, "But, you know, once you came down the rope, your hair was like, *completely* messed up, like, *beyond* belief." She looked at me, waiting for my response.

"Yeah, I know," I replied, "A giant fan with more power than a jet engine will do that to a person. Your own hair didn't look so hot after your run either, you know."

At that, Suzy shaped her mouth into a little 'o' and stared at me blankly. "I was just trying to let you know, so you, like, wouldn't be embarrassed, but then you, like, go all off on me for like, no reason at all."

And with that, Suzy turned on her heel and marched off toward her locker, blowing a bubble along the way.

"She seems to be in a good mood." Scarlet chimed.

"Yup, she didn't say anything about my 'hideous choice of footwear' this time." I replied, quoting Suzy's opinion on my tennis shoes that she so kindly shared with me last week.

"Forget about her, you know that if you're in a jam tomorrow Suzy will be right there beside you to help get you out, and the other way around too." Scarlet said as she stuffed the last of her clothes into her gym locker.

"True." I replied, thinking that she had read my mind about James. And the reality is, that *was* true: no matter how we treat each other at Henderson, we'll always be there for one another, no matter what. That's what makes the Henderson spy program so successful: We never give up on our fellow peers.

Even if those peers happen to love chewing gum and twirling their blond hair with perfectly manicured fingers.

Once Scarlet and I were all packed up, we set out for AP Chemistry, the PhD version. We were getting our books out of our adjacent lockers as the halls flooded with high school students. They all scampered off towards their next class, the non-spies completely oblivious to the new course record that had just been set on a military-grade obstacle course the period before.

"Kay! Scarlet!" A voice from 25 paces behind us called. Instinctively, Scarlet and I glanced at the closest reflective surface, but then remembered that the hall was filled with normal high school teens. There was no need to go into spy-mode there, so we turned towards the voice instead.

"Hey, Ted!" I called back, raising my hand in a wave at the boy approaching us.

In approximately 4.13 seconds, Ted Matthews had closed the space between Scarlet and I and himself as he bounded up to us.

Ted was of average height with light brown hair and equally light brown eyes. He had had a crush on Scarlet since 7th grade, but he was too scared to make a move. Scarlet claimed that Ted's crush was nonexistent, but she knew deep down that it was real. Ted was a sweet guy, if a little awkward at times.

"Guess what day it is?" Ted asked, a loopy grin plastered on his freckled face.

"Wait, don't tell me… Tuesday??" Scarlet taunted as she slipped her *Chemical Processes and You* textbook into her backpack.

"Well… yeah… but no! Mr. Needlemeyer promised something extra… *scienc-ey* today. But no one knows what it is! Do y'all have any idea?" Ted asked.

"Hmm…" I pressed my lips together in thought as I closed my locker and set off for AP Chemistry.

"Maybe we're finally going to be making that *special* fluid for that *thing* we learned about last week."

Mr. Needlemeyer had taught us about an ancient potion made from apple juice and the honey of a rare bee that will put anyone, and I mean *anyone* to sleep instantly. I'm talking Sleeping-Beauty-like sleep. It wore off after 24 hours, but after even a drop was sipped you were out cold.

"Maybe…" I could practically see the gears in Ted's head spin and churn as he thought this theory over. "But I'm not sure…"

"Well, I guess we're about to find about aren't we?" Scarlet said as she reached for the handle of the Chem Lab door and pulled.

What I saw before me was something I totally wasn't expecting.

"Please take your seats as we wait for the rest of the class, Miss Verdant, Miss Claire, and Mr. Matthews. You won't want to waste a millisecond of your time for what I have planned for today." Mr. Needlemeyer said as he leaned against his desk. In a leather jacket. And leather pants. And leather boots. Complete with a leather bandana around his neck. And black sunglasses on top of his head.

I think it goes without saying that this was the last thing I expected to see walking into Chem today.

Within the next 2 minutes and 16 seconds the entire 4th period sophomore Chemistry class was seated and anxious for today's lesson. Whatever it was, it had to be interesting for Mr. Needlemeyer to be clad in 90% leather.

"Ladies and gentlemen, today we learn the art of skill, strategy, and finesse when transporting a critical substance across a city. Ladies and gentlemen, today we create that critical substance using nothing but the materials found in the uppermost left cabinet. Ladies and gentlemen, the formal instructions to your assignment can be found in the bottom right drawer of my desk. Ladies and gentlemen, I wish you good luck."

And with that, Mr. Needlemeyer slipped his black shades on and began to head for the exit.

"Wait!" Ted called to our teacher, halting him in his abandonment attempt.

"Yes, Mr. Matthews?" Mr. Needlemeyer asked, clearly impatient.

"Umm... well... Uh, I mean no disrespect sir, but, uh... Why are you dressed like that?" Ted wrung his hands together as he awaited our teacher's response.

Mr. Needlemeyer simply smiled and continued walking out the door as he said, "Because I'm the one you need to keep the substance away from. This was just a taste of the different disguises I have up my sleeve. Out there, I could be anyone."

He closed the door behind him as he called over his shoulder, "Have fun."

It was shaping up to be your typical Tuesday afternoon at Henderson High.

Chapter Two

3 0 minutes later, with our newly-concocted potions con-
cealed in our backpacks, the sophomore class signed out
at the front office and set off for the Town Square, where Mr.
Needlemeyer's directions had instructed us to meet him.

"So... now what?" Ted asked, rubbing his hands together in
preparation for what we were about to do.

"Mr. N said to wait 10 minutes before making a move to
the convenience store on the left. What comes next should be
in there. So just be patient." Scarlet replied as she sat on a park
bench, face upturned in an attempt at a quick tan.

"Alright. If you say so." Ted said to Scarlet. I could practically
feel Scarlet tense from across the street.

"We have 4 minutes and 12 seconds left to wait before Flip-
Flop and I can make our move to the store." I said calmly from
across the street, pretending to admire some merchandise in a
store window. Not because I liked what was on sale, but because I
needed to maintain my cover as a normal high school girl.

The girl I was referring to as 'Flip-Flop' was actually a girl
named Sandra who was currently pretending to check out a de-
signer handbag in a shop window, the same way I was. She was
dubbed Flip-Flop because of her extensive collection and love of
various flip flops.

Everyone in the field, whether you were behind the scenes or
not, had a code name.

Mr. Needlemeyer had instructed that Sandra and I were to head over to the convenience store and pick up some packages of soda, which were supposed to contain supplies we would use to transport our concoctions to the old abandoned warehouse across the street.

The entire class was roaming around the town's main street in separate clusters so as not to raise suspicion.

Our cover was that we had just taken a huge AP Chemistry Exam, and the generous administration of Henderson High had decided to let us wander around our small town and relax for a while.

Several of my classmates' voices chattered in my ear through my centimeter long ear piece, each conversation different than the others.

For some people, all of those voices inside one head would drive them absolutely nuts; but it doesn't faze me one bit.

My older brother, Roy, always joked around with me that once I entered "spy mode", the teenage girl side of me was no longer present; it completely vanishes.

According to Roy, I become an android of spy-ness. I'm focused, analytical, determined, rough, and tough. Nothing stands in the way of me completing my mission. My mind is a database of what needs to be done and how to get it done. I complete my assignments with speed and efficiency, giving 120% in all that I do.

Those are his words, of course.

I can see his point though. I have to admit, I do become a tad bit more hard-core when I'm on a mission, and I can't help but let my eyes wander and analyze every millimeter of my situation. Call it training or genetics, spying is in my blood.

So when my internal timer rang that we had exactly 1 minute to get to where we needed to be, I nodded to Sandra and we strolled to the pharmacy next door.

Now, some of you might be wondering, 'Weren't they supposed to go to the convenience store?' Well, you're right, we were going to the store, just not directly.

Spying is all about *indirect* interaction. If you're going to take down a target in the middle of a packed town square, you don't just tackle them when everyone is watching (Our 8th grade Advanced Science teacher learned that the hard way). Instead, you tail them for a while pretending to be occupied, and when they're alone, *then* you can make your move.

Indirect action is in every spy's toolbox of skills, and the best spies know how to manipulate and utilize it to their advantage.

We wandered around like normal teenage girls, pretending to get distracted by the purses in the boutique window. But in reality I was on high alert, scanning every face in the square.

Mr. Needlemeyer could have been anyone. He said he would be watching us, waiting to make his move in stopping our assignment.

So when a middle aged man in a tracksuit stopped by a bench and stretched for 15.67 seconds, I indirectly observed.

When Sandra and I walked towards the pharmacy, I noticed a man in a navy suit and matching tie drive away in a beige car, so I memorized the license plate.

I wasn't going to take any chances.

Sandra and I pretended to admire some packaged cupcakes in the pharmacy window (I personally never understood why cupcakes were placed next to medicine) before crossing the street towards the convenience store.

We passed the store and continued on our way, until my internal clock signaled that time was almost up. So I cocked my head as a signal to Sandra.

Right on cue, Sandra exclaimed, "OMG! I totally forgot, my mom wanted me to pick up some sodas after school… what do you think about buying them now to save some time?" Her acting skills were flawless as she proclaimed her line, and I followed her lead.

"Sure! Look, the store is having a sale on soda, are we lucky or what?" And with that, we marched into the convenience store just as my clock hit zero.

"Afternoon ladies, what can I do ya for?" the sales clerk known only as Lizzie asked while she snapped her gum from behind the counter (Lizzie is her alias to the general public, none of my classmates know her real name).

Lizzie was a petite, fair skinned girl with gray eyes and black hair streaked with blue highlights. Everyone loved her, even though most of the youth in town didn't know her last name.

The interesting thing about Dulce, TX, is that the spy hospitality didn't end at Henderson High. Operatives were everywhere in Dulce, whether they were cashiers, doctors, construction workers, bankers, dentists, firemen, or just plain normal people. People of the spy breed were everywhere; we loved to hide in plain sight.

"Oh, we're here to buy some soda, is all." Sandra chimed at Lizzie as we walked past her.

"I've got some grape flavored soda here, it'll save you the trouble of walking to the back of the store." Lizzie replied.

I knew what she was doing. She was testing us, seeing if we would say the right thing. It was a classic spy move. You can never be too trusting.

"That depends Lizzie… what brand are they? We don't mean to be snooty, but the generic brand just doesn't have that… *zing* flavor we love." I smiled, knowing that I had said the right thing.

Lizzie smirked and then blew a bubble with her gum. "Oh, these have that *zing* all right. You can bet on that." She reached down under the counter and pulled out 3 cases of seemingly normal soda, except normal soda didn't have military-grade supplies hidden inside where a purple can should be.

"Those will do the trick! Thanks so much Lizzie! Oh, and could we get some chips, too?" I asked while Sandra was reaching for the soda.

"Absolutely. And for being so gosh darn nice, everything is on the house," Lizzie replied, throwing a wink in my direction, "You're welcome."

"Thanks so much Lizzie, you're the best!" I called behind my shoulder as Sandra and I walked out the door, soda and chips in hand.

Once we were out of Lizzie's earshot, Sandra whispered, "I

thought we were just getting soda."

"We were… but chips add to the cover. Besides, aren't you hungry?" I replied.

Sandra smiled at that.

Once outside of the store, Sandra and I wandered toward the gazebo with soda and chips in hand, while the rest of our classmates discreetly made their way towards the community center for Part 2 of our plan.

"Ok, we have the soda, and time seems to be on our side. Violet and Bear, you're a-go." I said in a low voice into my comms unit.

Scarlet, a.k.a Violet, and Ted, a.k.a Bear, heard my message in their ear pieces before getting ready to make their way towards us.

Within a few seconds, Scarlet and Ted had bounded over as Sandra chowed down on the chips from the store. I may have asked for them, but I wasn't going to distract myself from seeing suspicious activity.

"Hey, you guys!" Scarlet called cheerfully, ever the perfect actress.

"Hey Scar, what's new?" I sked, playing my own part.

Scarlet furrowed her brow in confusion. "What do you mean? Didn't you hear? Everyone is meeting up at the community center for a post-exam celebration. I thought you knew, since you have those cases of soda."

I mentally smiled, so as not to break cover. I was proud of the cover story my class and I had conjured up; Sandra and I would grab the soda while the rest of the class wandered around town, and when the time came to assemble the cases for our potions, we would all meet at the community center with a fake celebration as our cover up. From there we would make our way to the abandoned warehouse without letting Needlemeyer impede our plans.

"Oh, I didn't hear about that. Well, we could always take these to the party and go back for more later. After all, they were free!" Sandra said, rising to her feet to grab the cases.

"That's a good idea! C'mon, let's get going to the party." I said, throwing away the empty chip bag.

"Great! We can all go together." Ted beamed and gave a thumbs up before helping Sandra with the soda.

And then we were on our way to protect our potions.

Chapter Three

The walk to the community center wasn't very eventful, in terms of spy-related things, that is.

My classmates' voices continued to fill my ear as they made their own ways to the community center. The conversations consisted of normal teenage things, like allowances, driving, tests, and such. Our little foursome talked about those things as well. However, we also executed the standard counter-surveillance tactics to throw off anyone we might have had tailing us.

Instead of walking directly to the community center, we circled around some places before getting back on track. We took the long way of getting there, only to randomly turn and take a short cut in the process. We cut through the trees at one point, to better observe the people around us.

There were so many people walking around town, it was a little bit tricky to keep an eye on all of them at once.

A woman pushing a baby stroller kept stopping to adjust the diaper bag she had hanging from her shoulder.

An elderly man was sitting on a bench and tediously counting the pieces of bread he threw to each turtle dove that landed at his feet.

The elementary school a few blocks down didn't start dismissing students for another hour and a half, so I kept a sharp eye on two kids who were tugging at their mother's shirt asking for ice cream.

"You're sick, you can't have anything cold. Didn't you hear the doctor?" their mother asked.

Several more people passed by us, each with their own place to go and person to see.

After a few minutes, we passed the age-old playground that had been entertaining kids since the founding of Dulce itself.

That's when he caught my eye.

A man, in about his late 30's, was standing at the bus stop by the playground, and he kept glancing at his watch anxiously. A briefcase was sitting on the ground, handle waiting to be grabbed. He pulled his wallet out of his inner coat pocket and pulled out what looked like a bus pass. It was clear: he was getting ready for the bus to arrive.

My gut was telling me to notice the similarities between this man and Mr. Needlemeyer, from his height to his body type. I decided to watch and see what unfolded.

A woman emerged from the coffee shop down the street, holding a shopping bag in one hand and a cell phone in the other; she was tapping at her phone when she walked up to the bus stop. She and the man nodded a hello to each other as the woman set her bag onto the ground.

I can't tell you why, but my instincts were telling me to watch the two. There was something about their movements, their posture, their stance. There was something about them that seemed off to me.

I extended my hand ever so slightly, so that Scarlet would feel me brush her arm.

Her arm tensed at my spy-signal touch and she turned to look at me.

I gestured with my eyes towards the man and woman at the bus stop to my right, and Scarlet glanced at the shop window behind me, to see the reflection of the pair.

My internal clock told me that the 2:15 bus was going to arrive in a few minutes, and I had to see what the man and woman were going to do.

I knew that all four of us couldn't have stuck around to watch what unfolded; it was too suspicious.

"Hey, Sandra? Ted? Scarlet and I will meet you at the community center. There's something I have to do before I get there." I smiled as if to ask, *is that ok?*

Sandra and Ted gave me confused looks, so I mouthed the words *trust me* to give them assurance.

Sandra smiled and nodded before saying, "Sure. See you guys there."

She and Ted continued the journey towards the community center while Scarlet and I held back.

Once Sandra and Ted had walked for a while, Sandra's voice was in my ear.

"Asterisk, what was that about?" She asked, using my code name.

"I spotted a man and woman at the bus stop, both with bags and eager hands. Something seemed off to me. Violet and I will watch them to see if something is going on." I answered.

The rest of my classmates' voices were silenced as they listened in on the conversation.

"Well, you usually are right about things like this. I trust you." Sandra said firmly.

"As do I. Do you think it's The Subject?" Ted asked with a level voice. (The Subject was Mr. Needlemeyer, in case you were wondering.)

"I'm not sure Bear, but we'll keep you updated." I answered.

And with that, Scarlet and I walked over to the shop behind the bus stop to watch the waiting pair.

As soon as 2:15 rolled around, the bus pulled up to the stop. The woman looked up from her phone expectantly as the man bent down to pick up his briefcase.

It was easy to miss.

If I had blinked I would have missed it.

But I didn't.

I watched as the man picked up his briefcase by the handle and discreetly dropped the "bus pass" into the woman's shopping bag.

Seconds after the drop, the woman's phone rang.

"Hello?" She asked into the receiver as the man boarded the bus.

"Are you serious? Right now? Ugh, I'll be right over." The woman irritably hung up her phone, picked up her shopping bag, and walked away from the bus stop, where the man had already taken his seat.

I turned to Scarlet, who was wide eyed.

"Are you thinking what I'm thinking?" I asked in a hushed tone.

Scarlet nodded and grinned mischievously. "I take the Mr., you take the Ms.?" She asked.

"Definitely." I agreed.

And with that, we parted ways and began to follow our subjects.

Chapter Four

The woman wasn't the best agent in the world.

She never once executed counter-surveillance tactics, and she kept her eyes glued to her phone the entire time she was walking.

I followed at a discreet distance, mentally memorizing her habits.

She would tap, tap, tap at her phone, and only look up when something on her screen was loading.

She tucked her hair behind her ears a lot; it was always un-loosing itself.

She seemed to know exactly where she was going, since she was never looking around to see where she was.

Eventually her phone rang, and she stopped to answer it. But that didn't mean I had to stop.

I kept walking, even though I was closing the distance between us. It would have looked a bit off if she stopped and all of a sudden I did too. Instead, I walked over to a bench on the other side of the street and pretended to be taking pictures of the birds in the trees with my phone.

From my new surveillance spot, I could hear her conversation rather clearly. At first she was calm, saying that she was almost at the office, and that "the matter" would be resolved shortly. She became slightly irritable as she griped about having to deal with this on her day off.

She continued walking as she rambled on, and the conversation wasn't especially interesting. After a few seconds I rose from my seat and continued to follow her; she still seemed to not notice me.

I patiently waited for the right time to swipe the object the man had dropped in her shopping bag.

My chance came when she walked up to Jo Jo's Insurance and said into her phone receiver, "I'm here. I'm opening the door now... Yeah, see you in a bit."

And with that, I made my move.

I walked up to the Insurance Agency doors just as the woman did. She gave a quick smile to me as she reached for the door handle.

"Please, allow me." I said as I held the door open for her.

"Oh, why thank you!" She smiled at me again as she maneuvered her way through the front door.

I waited for the perfect moment, the exact timing needed to strike. She was right in front of me, her shopping bag swinging in her hand. When she was halfway past me, I slipped my hand into her bag and covertly felt for what the man had left in her bag.

She was about to feel the tug of my arm in her bag, so I had to act quickly.

After what felt like an eternity, (but was actually 2.4 seconds) I had the card and pulled my hand out of her bag.

I followed her into the building and strolled over to the clerk I knew, Mrs. Clasby.

"Hi, Mrs. C. My mom sent me in to ask about those emails she's been getting about 'going paperless'. She prefers to have things... *like the good old days.* You know?" I smiled my sweetest smile at her.

"*Like the good old days*" was a common spy term agents used to let another spy that they were on a mission or assignment.

Luckily, Mrs. Clasby had been an agent for as long as I could remember, and she knew the spy language backwards and forwards. Her and my mother had graduated from high school the same year, and knew each other pretty well. It was safe to use her as part of my cover.

"Sure thing, Kay. I'll make the change right now." She grinned sincerely and pretended to edit my mother's account. (It might have seemed odd that she was doing so, since none of our insurance was covered by Jo Jo, but none of the other clerks seemed to notice.)

"Thanks so much!" I told her.

I kept an eye on the woman, who disappeared into the back of the office. When she had first walked in she gave a gruff hello to the clerks up front and kept talking towards the back. There was no use for me to follow her. I had gotten what I wanted.

I slipped the card into my pocket.

"Well, I'm in a bit of a rush, so I've got to get going, but thanks again for the help!" I waved as I walked towards the door.

"No problem, and say hi to your mom for me!" Mrs. Clasby called after me.

"Will do!" I said cheerfully before leaving the building.

I wanted to whip the card out of my pocket right then and see that it was, but that wasn't an option. I had to wait.

I walked away and towards the bench I had been sitting at earlier.

"Asterisk, we've almost arrived at the community center. Anything you want to report? We heard your run in with 'Mrs. C.'" Sandra's voice was in my ear through my comms unit as I sat down at the bench.

"Yes, I have a status update. I saw a man and woman suspiciously standing at the local bus stop, and when he bent down to pick up his briefcase, he planted a card into the woman's shopping bag. I pursued the woman and managed to get my hands on what he dropped inside. I'm reading it now." I replied.

"Nice one, Kay. Uhm, I mean, Asterisk." Ted quickly correctly himself.

I read the contents card silently to myself, and as I did so, Scarlet's voice filled my ear.

"I tailed the man both on the bus and off, and I also performed a one sided brush pass, but he was clean. He has nothing on him." Scarlet sounded so disappointed I wanted to hug her, but I couldn't. I was all the way across town, so how could I?

I continued to read the card that said:

If you are reading this then congratulations, you have succeeded in my false test. Originally, you were asked to transport your substances to the abandoned warehouse discussed in my instructions. However, since you were clever enough to spot my drop, follow the receiver, and snatch this card, you were able to learn about this false test. Instead of delivering the substances to the warehouse, I want the entire class back at school before 3:15, where I will review and analyze the skills exhibited today. If even one student makes it to the warehouse due to lack of communication, the test is failed. If you are reading this, then an A+ is within your grasp. If, not, that's unfortunate. -Mr. N

"Guys, cancel the trip to the warehouse. Make sure everyone knows. This card says that the entire op was a sham. It was a test to see if we would spot the drop and pursue the subjects. *No one* can go to the warehouse, we need to get back to school before 3:15." I said into my ear piece.

My classmates grew quiet in my ear as they listened in to my explanation, and in no more than 2.4 seconds I heard the movement of my classmates packing up and getting ready to head back to school.

"Alright, Asterisk. I'm still across town from where I tailed the man, but I can meet you at the square so we can head back together." Scarlet told me.

"Sounds like a plan. Flip Flop, is everyone accounted for?" I asked Sandra.

"All but you two. We'll meet with you at school. Luckily, no one has gotten to the warehouse yet."

"Good. See you there." I told her before setting off with a spring in my step to meet with Scarlet.

It felt good to get an A.

Chapter Five

*a*fter heading back to school and receiving an A+ for getting my hands on the card, the school day was over and it was time to head home.

I usually walked back with Scarlet and we parted ways when we walked by her house on the way to mine.

She only lived about 2 blocks away, so the solitary walk to my own home wasn't that long.

I waved bye to her as she walked up her porch steps and I set off to my own abode.

I spotted the navy blue Mustang in the drive way of my house and knew my brother was home.

That Mustang was my brother's pride and joy. He got the 2007 sports car for the unbelievable price of $12,000, which he paid for himself.

Personally, a Camaro is my dream car; my brother and I were constantly arguing over which was better. (The Camaro was, obviously.)

I opened the door with my house key (the neighbors would have been a tad bit suspicious if they had seen me pick the lock with a stick I found on the ground) and headed straight for the kitchen.

"I'm hoooome!" I called to my big brother as I set my backpack down on a chair.

Roy came into the kitchen from the living room and ruffled my hair.

"Hey, Runt. I'm here. What's new?" He asked, using his pet nickname for me.

"I got an A in Chemistry for figuring out that our original assignment was a fake." I replied, fixing my brown hair in the mirror we had on our fridge.

My hair was shoulder length, with my side bangs framing my face, and I usually had it up in a ponytail. My green eyes stared back at me in the mirror, shining a little at my earlier accomplishments.

"Nice. I remember Mr. Needlemeyer. Always tricking us in some way or other." Roy said as he rummaged through the pantry.

Roy had just graduated from Henderson the year before as valedictorian. He was always trying to give me advice on what I should and shouldn't do, and was always reminiscing in his own school memories.

He was tall, strong, and lean, with hair the exact same shade of brown as mine, although his eyes were blue. Everyone in my household had brown hair, but my dad and I were the ones with green eyes while my mom and Roy had blue. Roy was always in a joking kind of mood, but he was as strong as a rock when it came to being serious. He loved to tease me, but I knew he meant nothing by it.

"Speaking of school... Any news from Lenox?" I asked hopefully.

Roy's expression grew disappointed as he grudgingly said, "No. Not yet. I've been checking all day."

I felt sorry for my brother. He had applied to study and continue his career as an operative at Lenox University of Covert Operations, one of the most prestigious (and not to mention secret) spy universities in the world. He hadn't heard word on whether or not he was accepted yet. They were supposed to send an email that would self-delete after 24 hours of being opened.

"Well... I'm sure you'll hear something soon!" I told him, trying to sound upbeat.

"Yeah. Whatever you say, Kay." He replied.

He headed back to the living room with a bag of potato chips in his hand, and I knew he was stress eating. I bit my lip. It irritated me when he did this; Roy was usually working out with me in his free time and was always trying to stay in tip top shape.

Seeing him pig out always worried me.

He must have tapped into our sibling telepathy and sensed what I thought, because he called from the living room, "Don't even think about lecturing me about these chips. We can both agree that they're delicious."

"Fine..." I groaned and rolled my eyes as I opened the refrigerator door.

I grabbed a can of Mountain Dew and continued to search the fridge for a snack.

"Who ate the last mini 3 Musketeers?! I called dibs!!!" I exclaimed.

Between chip crunches I heard my brother say, "Oops," before popping another chip into his mouth.

I grabbed my backpack from the chair it rested on and stomped over to the living room. I then grabbed a single potato chip out of the bag in Roy's hands.

"Hey!" He exclaimed indignantly.

"Hi." I replied before eating the chip and plopping onto the couch next to him. (He was sitting on our recliner, in case you were wondering.)

He reached out his arms to wrap me in one of his signature revenge bear hugs, but years of surviving his sibling torment allowed me to know to duck and run.

"Get back here, you chip stealing Runt!" He called when he jumped over the recliner to catch me.

"I'm faster than you, remember? I thought you learned that the hard way in Santa Rosa when we were chasing those arms dealers," he said, running after me throughout the bottom floor of the house.

"I'm better at evasive maneuvers. I thought you would have known, considering what happened in Stockholm when I outwitted the rogue agents and you didn't!" I called back to him.

"Oh, now you're in for it! You should know better than to

bring up that mission!" He yelled.

And with that, he dove for me, sliding on the carpet in an attempt to catch me by the ankles.

I easily moved out of the way, and plopped myself onto Roy's back. "Dog pile!" I yelled, laughing and smiling at my victory.

"Oh, you think you've won?" He asked mischievously.

He rose from the ground easily, even with my added weight. He held me up on his back, and I squealed for him to put me down.

"Whatever you say, Kay." He said before tossing me onto the sofa.

"You're so mean to me." I told Roy sarcastically while getting up from where I had been thrown.

He sat back down on the recliner and picked up his chip bag.

"I'm not the one who stole a chip, now am I?" He asked.

"No, but you did pick me up and throw me on the couch, thanks for that by the way." I replied.

Roy smiled one of his big brother smiles and continued eating.

I began to tackle my mountain of homework with a few sips of soda here and there as Roy flipped through the channels on the T.V.

He periodically went into the kitchen and grabbed new snacks, and upon his returns I chided him on his junk food habit.

He would then point out my fondness of all kinds of soda, and I would say something along the lines of "Touché". (Okay, "fondness" is an understatement. Roy's actual words were "an unhealthy addiction".)

After a while my mom came home from her job as a nurse at the local hospital. That was her cover career, of course. She was a spy just like my brother, father, and myself.

I've said it before, call it training or genetics, but spying has been with me since the womb.

"Hi, Mom!" My brother and I called from our positions in the living room as she walked through the front door.

My mom, Sylvia Jane Verdant, had brown, wavy hair that she loved to put into different styles for every different occasion. She was always so focused and strong, it made me want to grow up to be just like her. She had a fierceness to her personality that allowed her to take down bad guys with swiftness and ease. She was the best operative and woman I had ever met.

"Hey, kids. Kay, how was school?" She asked as she put her purse and keys on the coffee table.

"It was good. Mrs. Clasby says hi. I saw her while we were in town on an assignment today." I replied.

"Ooh, sounds fun," she said as she headed for the kitchen to cook dinner.

"Any word, Roy, sweetie?" She asked my brother, referring to his application to Lenox.

"No," he said quietly before eating the popcorn he had recently brought in.

"Honey, if you keep stress eating like that you'll run out of food and then you'll be even *more* stressed." My mom told him.

"I'm willing to take my chances," he replied.

Roy caught my eye and a thought passed between us.

"Do you need any help?" We asked my mom at the same time. Roy and I both knew that asking was pointless; my mom was always moving around and doing something productive. We wouldn't be able to keep up with her.

"Aw, you guys are sweet, but no thanks, I got this." She replied.

She pulled a pearl barrette out of her hair and, without looking, tossed it at a perfect angle into the jewelry dish she kept at the edge of the counter. It landed perfectly, of course.

My mom started to cook dinner, in preparation for my dad arriving home from his "construction job". He usually got home within 20 minutes of my mom's own arrival.

After a while, my mom called from the kitchen, "Dinner's ready!" Not more than a second after she told us, the front door opened and Parker Verdant (my dad) waltzed into the house.

"Good afternoon my lovely wife, my beloved daughter, and my awesome son." He bellowed from the front door.

"Afternoon, Dad!" Roy and I called to him.

My dad walked into the kitchen first and gave my mom a hug,

despite being covered with dust, soot, and sweat.

Personally, I loved how my father came home from work. The mud and paint marks were proof of how hard he worked all day, and it made me proud to see symbols of his handiwork when he came home.

My dad walked into the living room to greet us next, clapping Roy on the back and saying hello, then giving me a hug from behind the couch.

"Hi, Daddy. What's up?" I asked.

My dad straightened from the hug he had given me, and pulled off his cap. His brown hair was damp and stuck up at odd angles due to his sweat. My father was a hardworking man with a loving heart and sharp intellect. His tough build added to his strength and speed he displayed on missions. His green eyes twinkled in the way they did when he had something important to tell us, so I knew that he had something on his mind.

"Well, approximately 2.6 minutes before I got out of the car and came into the house, I got a call from O.U.O (Organization of Undercover Operatives). They want us to help provide security at The Senatru Art Museum in Europe. They suspect that one of the exhibits is going to be robbed. With the robberies that went underway at other museums in surrounding states, they're under-staffed. We leave in the morning," he announced.

And with that, Roy and I jumped up from our comfy spots and high-fived each other.

"Alright! Road trip!!" We exclaimed.

My dad extended his hands out, palms down in an attempt to calm us down.

"Easy, easy, it's just 2 days, and we're there to make sure that nobody breaks in while they install new security at certain exhib-its," my dad explained.

"Still... Road trip!" My brother cheered.

I smiled at my brother's enthusiasm. It felt good to see him in his usually upbeat mood.

"You hear that, Mom? Road trip! To Europe!" I said as I walked into the kitchen.

My mom finished placing plates of spaghetti onto the kitchen table and smiled at my dad, brother, and me.

"Well, then we better finish dinner fast so we can start packing!" She said cheerfully.

We all smiled and sat down as we enjoyed our family meal.

Afterwards, my dad called Mr. Johnson, the principal of Henderson High (who was also a spy), to let him know I would be gone for the next few days. When missions like this came up, the school used the cover story that students were on academic or sporting retreats, so as not to raise suspicion on why students were gone so long and frequently.

After packing, I walked to Scarlet's house and told her about the mission in Europe.

"Aw, you're so lucky!" She said when I finished explaining the gist of my mission. I couldn't tell her all the details before the official debriefing report was written and submitted. All I could say was that I was heading to Europe for a while, and I promised to tell her all the juicy details once it was ok.

I loved the fact that Scarlet understood living the life of a spy. We never got annoyed with each other when protocol got in the way, and we loved to tell our stories to one another.

She wished me good luck when I left her house, and I hardly got any sleep that night.

It had been 5 months since my last mission abroad, and I was excited to visit a different continent again. Not that the missions in my own country weren't fun, but being in a whole new environment had a certain *danger* vibe that I loved.

Little did I know, that mission would change my life, for both better and worse.

Chapter Six

Many hours later, I was securing the perimeter of The Senatru Museum with Roy while my parents covertly discussed what security measures were going to be changed with the Heads of Security. (The fact that the conversation took place behind 3 locked doors and soundproof walls was not declared for the public to know. Then again, neither was our being there...)

Once the perimeter was secured, Roy and I decided to split up; he would survey the scene outside the museum while I took a look around on the inside.

"Be careful, Runt. I'm here on comms if you need me." He assured.

To prevent any excess noise or feedback on our comms unit, we had our comms on manual mode, where we had to physically touch the earpiece to speak into the open conversation.

It was a good idea, and I always felt a lot more spy-like when I spoke into the unit that way.

"Ok, and you be careful too. Who knows what can happen out here?" I replied.

Roy laughed. "Please. What could go wrong on a day like this? Wait, I think that squirrel just looked at me funny..."

I whacked my big brother on his arm before heading off inside the museum, leaving his laughter behind me.

I'm not going to lie, the museum was gorgeous.

The intricate carvings in the stone ceiling framed the dazzling chandeliers that hung overhead.

Just the right mix of soft and bright light shone from vintage lamps illuminating statues and paintings.

Floor to ceiling pillars of alternating marble and granite were placed throughout the wings of the museum, providing an elegant feel.

Golden ivy with brass accents climbed up the pastel walls, shining when the light hit them at just the right angle.

The cherry colored hardwood floors were worn from use, but still sturdy enough to be classy.

Several brown leather benches with golden studs sat around, providing a quick resting stop for anyone who wanted to sit and admire a piece of art.

I strolled around the main entrance, admiring every detail of the museum decor. But I wasn't there to get the interior decorator's phone number (even though it would have been a smart idea).

Instead, I walked around, stopping to admire each work of art in several of the different sections.

As I did so, I mentally memorized how many steps it was from one door to another (an average of 156), how many public and hidden security cameras were in each room (50 in the main entrance, 35 in every other room), and how many potential points of entry and exit were available in each section (24, not including air ducts. With them, it was 38).

I was aware that the East Wing was currently closed while employees and my father ran tests to ensure that the system wouldn't malfunction while other security measures were installed in the wing next to it later on.

I wasn't worried about anyone breaking in while my father was on patrol; he had an insanely awesome spy sense and equally amazing spy skills that had helped him complete missions so epic neither my brother nor I had the clearance to hear the stories (We were really close though!).

Even so, I kept an eye on the direction of the East Wing, taking into account who went that way, how long they took, and how disappointed and/or irritated they were when they came back. (One man stomped to the front desk and demanded to know why his favorite wing was closed off. Needless to say, I paid special attention to him.)

There were a lot of people drifting in and out of sections of the museum, and some were entering and leaving the museum entirely.

I registered every one of their faces in my mental database, taking into account where they went, what they did, and what they wore.

A man with a cane, monocle, trench coat, and top hat was taking the time to admire each and every statue the museum displayed.

A young couple, each with wedding bands on their left ring fingers, would stop to look at several different paintings, and every time they did so, the woman would rest her head on the man's chest and the man would make a comment on whatever they were looking at.

A woman with purple hair, torn skinny jeans, and combat boots gravitated towards the abstract pieces.

A family of three, who were obviously tourists, treated every step in the museum as a new experience.

The father of the family took pictures of everything he possibly could, while the mother consulted the museum map she picked up at the front desk.

The child of the trio was a boy who seemed to be about 7 years old. He carried a brown burlap-like bag with paint brushes sticking out of it, and he proudly declared the artist of every painting he saw.

I couldn't help myself. At the sight of them, I smiled.

They were a normal family taking a normal vacation to this museum to enrich their son's love of art.

My family was *not* normal, our vacation was *not* normal, and the only reason we were here was to help increase security and potentially take down any art thieves we came across.

Honestly, I wouldn't want it any other way.

I continued observing the museum around me, taking note of the details.

After approximately 22.47 minutes, the East Wing was re-opened and my father and the employees left the area.

As they walked out, my father passed right by me, and we both pretended not to notice each other.

After a few seconds, I heard his voice in my ear, "Security checks in East Wing are complete, the next system reboot won't be until after hours. Kids, keep a sharp eye out until then, clear?"

"As crystal." Roy and I said at the same time.

"Poet, is your observation point proving to be useful?" Roy asked using my mom's code name.

My mom was currently across the street with high powered binoculars, a camera with a 1000x zoom, and a tablet to take notes, all way up high at a hidden surveillance spot on top of the roof of a building.

From there, she could observe the entrances to the museum from afar safely and covertly.

"It sure is, Chief. I haven't seen any suspicious activity yet, but I'll keep you updated." She replied using Roy's code name.

"Alright, I'm heading over to meet Poet. Kids, you stay on the premises to check for anything out of place." My dad told us.

"Roger that, Handy Man." Roy and I replied to my dad.

I was proud of my parents and brother; with the entire Verdant Family on the job, who knows what we were capable of.

After our brief spy-to-spy conversation, I returned to the

mission at hand.

Several people made their way into the East Wing, eager to see what they had been shut out from.

I myself wandered into that section, which was filled with beautiful landscape paintings.

I found myself admiring a few, not because it was a part of my cover, but because I was genuinely interested.

I drifted from one painting to another, falling more and more in love with the majestic mountains and rolling plains.

Then I saw him.

Oh, when I saw him.

He had such an impact on me, I was physically halted.

I involuntarily stopped short, and I couldn't help but think that if Roy were there, he would mock me for abruptly stopping like an amateur.

My knees went weak, so weak that I was seriously scared I was going to fall over.

The boy was tall and lean, with subtle, yet noticeable muscles. There was no doubt in my mind that a six pack hid behind his leather jacket.

His hair was a dusty brown, with the slightest traces of blond peeking through. He had it in the perfect style where it stuck up in all the right places without being messy.

He seemed fascinated by the floral pasture he was admiring; he never took his eyes off of it.

I don't know why I paid so much attention to him.

None of the other people in the museum had made me stop and stare.

I can't quite tell you why, but my gut was telling me that somehow he was different. I could tell that he wasn't like the other visitors. For some reason, I felt that he was special. That he was... like me.

I casually strolled over to a painting a little ways off from where he was.

I could see him in my peripheral vision, and his reaction to my own presence was notable.

I saw him glance my way and falter.

He took a step back and bumped into a pillar, which he coolly leaned against to recover.

He crossed his arms, then put his hands in his pockets, then crossed his arms again, as if he didn't know what to do with his hands.

He watched me for a few seconds, then turned back to his painting.

I couldn't understand why he had reacted that way.

I mean, there wasn't anything particularly special about me.

I wasn't incredibly tall or insanely pretty; my jean capris, ankle boots, and navy T-shirt didn't exactly scream, "LOOK AT ME."

I figured that the only way to find out why I felt so drawn to him was to put my mind on cruise control and let myself walk towards him.

I just didn't know that by doing so, I was sentencing myself to a whirlwind of drama and experiences I never could have imagined.

Chapter Seven

I had never understood why girls drooled over boys or why they let themselves revolve around the male species so intensely.

The "girl meets boy" love story didn't really seem probable for someone in my profession.

I was supposed to be strong, focused, and always on top of my mission. There was no time for swooning over cute boys in museums.

My mom and dad had met on a mission and fell in love over time, but that's a once in a lifetime story you either experience yourself or hear about from people you know.

I seriously doubted it could happen to me, too.

I decided to just stop worrying and go for it; I figured if I was able to stare down big time bad guys, I could face a seemingly harmless boy.

Walking up to that particular boy though, I felt millions of years of sophisticated female evolution simply spiral down the drain.

Being there a few feet away from him, all the confidence and self-composure I usually possessed was gone, and I had absolutely no idea how to get it back.

I decided to wing it.

I calmly walked up to the painting he was looking at and stopped to admire it just as he was.

We stood like that for a few minutes, silently looking at the painting.

It was a large landscape depicting a rolling hill covered with colorful dahlia flowers. Each a different size and shape, the flowers were so life-like, and the artist managed to give them a sun kissed glow.

I was mesmerized by the beauty captured with a canvas and paintbrush, and I could tell the boy was too.

After what felt like an eternity, he spoke.

"It's amazing, isn't it?" He asked coolly (with an American accent, I might add), turning to face me.

I smiled and replied, "It really is."

I looked back at him and practically melted when warm, vibrant hazel eyes looked back at me.

The boy smiled at me, and I tried my very hardest not to swoon.

"I mean, the way the artist managed to paint every detail of every single flower, all while keeping with the rolling hill effect... It's just amazing." Hazel Eyes studied the painting for a few seconds before turning back to me. "You know?" He asked.

"I do." I replied, continuing to admire the landscape.

I continued, "The way they seem to sway in the breeze while standing still in the real world is incredible too. The whole thing just..."

"Takes your breath away." He finished for me.

I turned to face him, and as he looked back at me I felt something coursing between us.

I can't tell you exactly what it was, but I felt a connection with him, as if we both had something buried beneath the exterior, and we could sense it in each other.

We stood like that for a little bit, looking at each other, trying to decipher the unusual bond between us.

Eventually, after not being able to figure it out, Hazel Eyes leaned against the pillar and crossed his arms, the epitome of cool.

"So..." He started, then trailed off when he realized I hadn't yet told him my name.

His eyes wandered around, as if my name would just be floating in midair. His gaze drifted to the painting, and a smooth smile spread across his lips.

"Delilah. You come here often?" He asked.

I giggled. Yes, giggled. "Delilah?" I asked, "Those are dahlias in the painting." I told him.

"True. But Delilah just sounds better. A pretty name for a pretty girl." He said in a casual, boy-ish tone.

I blushed, not knowing what to say.

I've said it before, I never understood why girls made such a fuss over boys.

Slowly but surely, I was finally starting to grasp the concept.

Hazel Eyes uncrossed his arms and put his hands in his pockets before saying, "By the way, Delilah, you never answered my question. You come here often?"

I smiled at him and replied, "Actually, no. This is my first time here."

It was the honest truth. Being a spy was half knowing when to tell the truth, and half knowing when to follow your cover.

In those moments, I was doing a little bit of both.

Hazel Eyes nodded and asked, "So, are you here with anybody?"

I had to follow my cover.

"My brother and I are visiting. We're kind of going through an art phase together, so we've been visiting museums and galleries left and right." I replied, my voice calm and even.

Hazel Eyes nodded again, but didn't say anything else.

"What about you?" I asked.

He smirked. "What about me?"

I cocked my head. "Do *you* come here often? Are *you* here with anybody?" I asked, trying to mask the smile on my lips.

He laughed a little before replying, "I've been here once before. A sculpture my dad had been dying to see was debuting here. Now I'm here alone. Just cruising around."

"Cool," I told him, smiling.

He smiled back.

I opened my mouth to continue, then realized something slightly terrifying.

The comms unit in my ear was emitting the most subtle trace of static, almost too soft to be heard.

But I did hear it.

Something was wrong.

When a comms unit made that sound, that means that the connection was down, and there was no way I could talk to anyone on the other side.

This particular model wasn't supposed to get caught up in interference or become distorted when one person was out of range.

Something, or someone, was jamming the signal.

I had to slip away from Hazel Eyes and find Roy, but just walking away without saying a word wasn't an option, and frankly, it was a little on the rude side.

I put together a plan in my head before saying, "Well, there are a lot of other pieces I want to see here, so-"

But I was cut off by two strong hands clasping down on my shoulders.

Needless to say, things were going to get interesting.

Chapter Eight

My first instinct was to grab the arms holding me, duck under them, turn, and pin their wrists between their shoulder blades.

But then their grip loosened, and they squeezed just the right spot on my right shoulder to activate a pressure point and make me squeal.

I turned towards the person behind me, embarrassed out of mind from yelping in front of Hazel Eyes, and found myself looking up at Roy.

"There you are. I was looking all over for you. Our bus leaves in like an hour, and we still need to see the exhibits in the North Wing." My big brother said, completely calm while playing his part.

I glanced down at my HoloWatch, which was currently disguised to look like one of those $200 smart watches and not a highly sophisticated operative tool.

"Aw, geez, I hadn't even noticed how much time had gone by. We better get going." I replied.

Roy nodded, then glanced at the boy next to me.

Hazel Eyes did that half nod thing that guys do to say hello to each other, and Roy just stared him down.

They stayed like that for a while, as if engaging in some secret staring contest.

I felt extremely awkward, so I grabbed Roy's hand and began to pull him towards the direction of the exit.

I turned to Hazel Eyes, who stopped looking at Roy and faced me.

He smiled as he said, "I guess you'll be going then. I'll see you around."

"Hopefully," I said, smiling back.

Hazel Eyes laughed at that and replied, "Yeah. Hopefully."

He turned towards Roy and gave a sloppy two fingered salute, in an attempt to say goodbye.

Roy completely ignored him and pulled me along.

I stole one last glance at Hazel Eyes and mouthed the word, '*Sorry!*'

He smiled and mouthed back, '*It's ok!*' as our final goodbye.

I smiled back and continued walking with Roy.

Once we were out of earshot, I said, "Ok. First, what you pulled back there was really rude, and second, why is the comms link down?"

We continued to head for the exit without breaking pace as Roy replied, "First, I was not rude, I was being an older brother. You're fifteen. I'm supposed to treat every guy you meet badly, it's a part of the job. Second, I have no idea. The static came on, and I knew it was useless to try and reach Mom and Dad. So I came looking for you."

We left the East Wing and detoured to the main entrance.

"First, I really don't see how being rude to a guy you've never met is part of the older brother job description. Second, I had the same thought. I was about to go find you when you grabbed me in the East Wing." I said.

"First, you shouldn't question the older brother way of doing things. I am your older brother, after all. Second, let's just head across the street to the surveillance spot where Mom and Dad are. We'll figure things out there." He replied.

I nodded, letting the older brother comments slide... for now.

We executed short counter surveillance tactics before finally heading out of the museum.

We crossed the street together, just two siblings on their way to get where they wanted to go.

We split up once we got to the other side, Roy heading left and myself heading right.

We walked for a while, then disappeared into alleys. From there we walked behind the buildings, and finally met up at the back of the building where my parents were.

We climbed the ladder leading from the ground to the roof, and found our parents packing up their equipment.

"What are you doing? What happened?" Roy asked.

"Comms are down, as I'm sure you've noticed. I don't know where the signal is coming from, but I'm positive it has to do with the suspected robbery. Your mother and I were packing up here so we could meet with you all back at the museum. We need to investigate this hands on." My father told us.

Right when he said, "I don't know," I was already activating my HoloWatch and trying to trace the signal.

I took the comms unit out if my ear and inserted it into a miniscule opening on my watch.

From there, the sound of static coming from the earpiece became more profound as it was emitted from the speakers on my watch.

The holographic screen grew in size as the comms unit information came up on screen.

I worked my way through dialogue boxes and punched in strings of code in an attempt to identify the source of the jam.

"Whoever's hacking our signal has experience. There are no obvious digital fingerprints that can lead me to them. They're good... But not good enough." I said, tapping at my screen.

After a few firewall bypasses, I triangulated the source of the jam.

"Got it! The signal is coming from the west, a laptop 2 blocks away is giving the order to jam and a signal amplifier is directing it to the museum." I announced to my family.

"Great work, Kay. Your father and I will go investigate the source, while you and Roy go tell the security consultant to pay extra attention to any personnel in and out of the museum." My mother told me.

"Runt and I can handle going to check out the source. If there's a security breach, you two are better equipped to handle it. Besides, the security guards at the museum probably take you guys more seriously than us." Roy said, trying to persuade our parents.

"You do have a point... But I know you just want to go where the action is." My father replied.

"Ok, there's that too," Roy agreed.

"Fine. You two go to the source, Kay, you'll try to disable it. Roy will be there to help you. Your father and I will run extra perimeter checks and have the security footage reviewed for any suspicious activity." My mom said.

"Sounds good." Roy and I replied at the same time.

"You two be careful, now." My mom said, coming over and giving both my brother and I a kiss on the cheek.

"You too." Roy replied.

"Good luck!" I chimed in.

And with that, Roy and I climbed down the building and set off through the shadows to find the source.

The laptop and amplifier ended up being in a dark alley behind an abandoned three story building.

Once we entered the alley, a serious, somber mood settled on both my brother and myself.

This was always one of the most suspenseful parts of the job; knowing what you're going in to do, but not knowing exactly what you're going to get.

We crept up to the scene cautiously, careful not to give away our positions.

Roy held his arm out behind him, the universal signal for "stay behind me".

I did as I was told, or well, gestured, and made sure not to get ahead of my big brother.

Roy slowly crouch-walked his way closer and closer to the source, and I silently followed behind.

The laptop and amplifier were at the very end of the dark alley, so Roy and I got a dimly lit view of what we were approaching.

There was no one near the laptop or the amplifier; they were operating on a continuous loop.

Roy signaled for me to turn on my HoloWatch, which I did immediately.

I started to run basic security bypasses, then got through to the laptop's amplifier extension. I started to figure out what type of signal was being emitted, managed to stop the signal, and replaced it with a similar one so that whoever put it here wouldn't be surprised over why *their* jamming signal was *being* jammed.

It was a lot less complicated than it sounded.

After a few minutes, the static in my comms unit disappeared, and Roy whispered, "Nice."

I whispered back, "Why, thank you kindly," and contacted my parents via the comms link.

"Testing whether or not the link is reestablished and functional, Poet and Handy Man, please respond." I softly spoke into my earpiece.

"This is Handy Man checking in." My father said, right before my mother said, "Poet here, the link seems to be operational."

"Good. The scene of the jam seems to be deserted, so Asterisk and I will move in straight to the source. From there we'll try to figure out who owns the equipment." My brother told my parents.

"Sounds like a plan," My mom replied, "Handy Man and I will continue working over here."

"Roger that." I told her.

Roy walked over to the laptop, cautious and careful not to trip any alarms that may have been set to protect the signal jammer.

I followed him and assessed the situation at the laptop.

The files that were meant to jam signals were one time use only; a classic move to prevent signals from being traced back once they were disabled.

The file that had initially been run had been labeled "Test_072536", and the one underneath was named "Official_739264".

I raised an eyebrow at Roy, who leaned over my shoulder to take a look.

We looked at each other, using our sibling telepathy to communicate.

I can't tell you why or how, but my brother and I could have entire conversations with a flicker of our eyes.

Roy gave me a look as if to say, "You know what this means right?"

I nodded as the pieces fell into place in my head.

Whoever had been jamming the signal was running a test to see if it would work.

That meant that whatever they were planning hadn't happened yet.

But it was going to.

I got into the laptop and checked for any cameras, voice recorders, or motion sensors that could have been the demise of my brother and myself, and luckily I found none.

I then tried to find any information leading to who owned the files and when they were going to strike.

The laptop was completely blank other than the audio files.

I was seriously disappointed that the laptop had given us absolutely no leads; I bit my lip as a result.

"Hey, we'll figure it out. Stop being so irritable." My big brother whispered to me.

"I'm not being irritable." I countered, starting to inspect the amplifier.

Roy rolled his eyes. "Yeah, you are. You bite your lip when you're annoyed, I've told you before." He said.

I bit my lip even more at his extensive sibling knowledge.

"This amplifier isn't giving me any details, and I doubt I have the time to trace where it was bought, when, and who bought it." I explained to him.

"Well, we can either sit here and wait for the owner to come back, or head back to the museum to help mom and dad." Roy said.

"Poet, Handy Man, anything to report?" I asked my parents through my comms unit.

"No activity, but the site is closing soon. Too soon. You two better get back here." My dad replied.

I glanced at Roy, who gave a single nod.

"Alright, we're heading over." I told him.

"This is going to be interesting." My brother said as we slipped out of the alley.

I replied, "We'll see."

Chapter Nine

$\mathcal{B}$ y the time Roy and I got back to the museum, the place was crawling with security personnel. Not enough for the public to be concerned, but enough for my family and I to notice.

Upon returning to the museum, my mom and dad had instructed my brother and I to split up and continue cruising around, on the lookout for anything suspicious.

"If you see anything, and I mean *anything*, you run to me and start talking, are we clear?" Roy asked me.

I nodded. "We're clear. Although, running to my spy brother and telling him details about our secret mission in the middle of a packed museum doesn't seem very spy-like." I told him.

Roy rolled his eyes at me. "You're crazy." He replied, giving me a warm, big brother smile.

And with that, we headed our separate ways.

The security guards seemed to be doing a very good job of keeping an eye on the entrances and exits, as well as the people in the wings.

I walked around the inside of the museum, admiring both the art works and the security team's surveillance tactics.

As I passed by a steel rack, I reached out and grabbed a map of the museum, free to all visitors.

I decided that it would be my souvenir for the mission; I always kept one for every op.

It felt good to stretch my legs as I wandered around the different wings, and I liked having something to do while waiting for the museum to close.

Finding the laptop and amplifier had definitely raised my suspicions, so I was extra wary and observant as I walked around the museum.

I was just about to turn down a hallway filled with pastel colored paintings when I spotted him out of the corner of my eye.

Hazel Eyes, looking just as good as the first time I saw him, was looking up at a particularly small sculpture.

The work of art depicted a bird about to take flight from a tree branch, and for some reason I found that both inspirational and suspenseful.

The thought of the bird taking off and soaring above the clouds was uplifting, but deep inside lay the unspoken fear that the bird would falter and crash.

The sculpture was mounted up on a wall, high above the museum goers' heads.

It may have been mistaken as a decoration, or just passed by without a second glance.

But for some reason, Hazel Eyes found it fascinating.

I watched as he stayed looking up at the bird, as if it would look down and talk to him at a moment's notice.

He had a pensive look on his face, and his eyes seemed distant, as if he were deep in thought.

I had to snap myself out of my creepy staring position and compose myself.

My mission was to keep the museum safe while new security measures were installed, not drool over a boy I had just met.

Even though that boy was suave, had eyes that you could swim in, a smile that would make you melt, and an adorable sense of humor...

He wasn't my mission.

Right now, I was supposed to be focused on keeping the museum safe, and now there was the added pressure of the laptop and amplifier.

As far as I knew, there were no potential operatives in the area, so it seemed especially odd that the laptop and amplifier were to just be left in the open.

I hated when something during a mission didn't add up, so you can bet that this bugged the heck out of me.

I mentally debated whether or not I should talk to Hazel Eyes, you know, to see if he had seen anything suspicious in the museum.

Yeah, that was a good reason to talk to him.

But then again, I had my mission.

I wasn't able to make a decision, though, because Hazel Eyes chose that exact moment in time to turn around and catch a glimpse of me.

He stopped in his tracks and smiled, so I smiled back.

He started to walk towards me, and I panicked a little bit.

After all, I was supposed to be on a *mission*. I had never before gotten so side tracked because of something, especially a hazel eyed boy.

He closed the distance between us and put his hands in his pockets before speaking.

"Well, odd to see you back. I thought you had to take the bus?" He pointed out coolly.

Luckily, I was a master at thinking on my feet.

"Oh, yeah. My brother and I missed the bus, so we're going to have to wait until the next one arrives. The museum is almost closing anyway, so we figured we might as well see as much art as we can." I replied.

Hazel Eyes nodded, and his eyes drifted back to the bird statue.

"What?" I asked, smothering the smile on my lips.

He flicked his eyes towards me, and gave a coy grin.

"What do you mean, 'what'?" He asked.

I jutted out my chin in fake annoyance.

"What is it about that statue that's so fascinating?" I inquired.

He grew quiet, and seemed to be deep in thought for a moment.

He did this thing with his lips, where he pressed them together slightly, but only at the left corner of his mouth.

It was one of the single cutest things I had ever seen in my life.

"Honestly... I don't know. It just... I don't know." He replied.

He glanced at me, and I could tell he was waiting to see my reaction.

I nodded my head and replied, "I know exactly what you mean."

It was the honest truth.

Sometimes, spy-life or not, you just... don't know.

Hazel Eyes smiled, and he opened his mouth to say something, but he was cut off.

"Excuse me, miss, you're going to have to come with me."

Under normal circumstances, I would have been *seriously* concerned with the voice directed to me.

Was I compromised? Had something happened? Did I fail my mission?

But luckily, I registered the voice as none other than my loving father, who was making his way towards me in a fancy security uniform.

Hazel Eyes looked over at the man, and for a split-second, nothing more, he looked like he wanted to bolt.

It was subtle, almost unnoticeable. Any other person probably would have missed it.

But I didn't.

He tensed the slightest bit, and his eyes widened, just barely.

He recovered in less than a second, in fact his change in composure lasted less than a second, but it was there.

I had seen it myself.

I looked at my dad coming towards me, and I pretended he was a stranger.

I wrinkled my brow as I looked up at him in confusion, and asked, "Is there a problem, sir?"

He adjusted his hat and replied, "I was given instructions by your brother to come find you. He is looking for you as well, at the entrance of the museum."

I nodded my head, knowing that since the museum was about

to close, it was time for some regrouping and debriefing.

"Ok, I'll go meet him right now. Thank you." I smiled to show my thanks, and he tipped his hat at me.

I tried my hardest not to give him a hug.

My dad glanced at Hazel Eyes for a single second before turning around and walking away.

"So, I guess you gotta go, again, huh?" Hazel Eyes asked.

"Yeah. My older sibling calls." I replied.

Hazel Eyes laughed and smiled at me.

"I'll see you around then, Delilah. Don't forget me." He said.

I laughed and replied, "Trust me, I won't."

He smiled once again, turned, and walked back towards the bird statue.

I turned around and walked towards the museum entrance.

I caught up with my dad, and together we met up with my mom, Roy, and the head of museum security to discuss the main security upgrade that was taking place in less than an hour.

Once the museum closed, Roy and I did routine perimeter sweeps and kept an eye out for any potential art thieves while my parents helped to install the security systems.

I was proud of our handiwork; the systems were put together with no problems at all, and Roy and I didn't see anything out of the ordinary the entire time they were working.

Once we were all finished up, we backtracked and headed to the alley where the laptop and amplifier had been.

They were nowhere in sight.

We checked the security cameras in the alley, but they revealed nothing.

After that, my family and I headed to our hotel room, where we peacefully slept after a good day's work.

The next day we went back to the museum to check on the security systems in action.

Everything ran smoothly.

I didn't see Hazel Eyes that day, and I have to admit, I was a bit disappointed.

Oh, well. I thought. *He was probably just a one-time thing.*

When the day was over, we went home, *real* home, back in Texas.

Everything was going pretty normally when we got back, and during the mission debrief we were told we did an excellent job.

After 4 days, we received word that a single item from the museum had been stolen.

It was so insignificant, museum workers didn't really know when it was taken.

They just know that somehow, it went missing.

The item stolen?

A particularly small statue depicting a bird about to take flight from a tree branch.

Chapter Ten

While the statue being stolen was odd, the museum told us not to worry about it.

It had been acquired after the owner went bankrupt and had to auction off some of their excess items.

The museum stated that no one would even notice, and they were probably right.

But I couldn't stop thinking about Hazel Eyes, and his fascination with the statue.

Maybe it was just a coincidence.

Maybe not.

All I know is that when I told my mom about it, she told me to just shrug it off.

My mom is one of the best operatives I know, so I trusted her.

If she thought that a cute boy who liked the statue shouldn't be under suspicion, then who was I to go against her advice?

Scarlet was a little more open than I was.

"Do you think he had anything to do with it?" She asked me, while we juggled soccer balls during PE.

"I'm not sure," I replied, mentally keeping count of my bounces (so far I was at 52), "he just seemed… different."

"Different how?" Scarlet asked, as she stopped juggling to kick her ball to me.

I quickly stopped juggling my own ball and stopped hers with my foot, then replied, "I can't really describe it. From the moment I saw him, he just seemed… *different*. There's no other word to describe him. It was almost like he was…"

"Like us?" Scarlet finished for me after I passed the ball back to her.

"Yeah," I replied, kicking up my ball and beginning to juggle again. "Like us."

Scarlet cocked her head while she thought. "Maybe-"

FFFFWWWOOOOT!!! Coach Oslo's whistle blew.

"Alright, enough with the juggling and surprise passing, let's see some stealing!" She ordered.

I quickly kicked my ball away and went straight for Scarlet, who fended me off really well.

"As you were saying," I told her.

"Maybe you just had a teensy little crush on him, so you felt that way. He could have nothing to do with it, you just feel that way because you liked him." She said, twisting and lunging to keep the ball out of my reach.

"Scar, how can I have a crush on someone I just met?" I asked, throwing out my foot and swinging it forward, perfectly stealing the ball away from her.

"Nice, Miss Verdant." Coach said as she walked by.

"I don't know, but you did." Scarlet replied, during a vain attempt to kick the ball out behind me.

"Well, whatever it was about him, he was different." I told her, trying to defend my case.

"So this guy… 'Hazel Eyes'… was he cute?" She asked.

"Scar!" I exclaimed, as she stole the ball away.

"What?" She played innocent, "It was just a question!"

I rolled my eyes as I tried to steal the ball back.

"You're crazy. Actually, correction, you're *boy* crazy." I replied.

"Say whatever you want about me, sticks and stones." She said.

"Uh, huh." I said, stealing the ball back.

Coach Oslo blew her whistle, and bellowed that class was over.

Once the class had put everything away, Scarlet and I headed for the locker room.

"Oh, and to answer your question," I told her, "Yes, he was

really cute."

"I knew it!" Scarlet grinned, teasing me with her smile.

Later that day, I was hit with a double whammy.

Once I got home, Roy told me that our parents had been called away for an op in South America, and they would be gone for a couple of days.

The fact that they had a mission didn't faze me; it was a part of the normal spy life.

The fact that they left without saying goodbye is what hurt.

They always found a way to say bye.

I guess this time, Roy was the messenger of farewells.

No sooner was I about to call Scarlet and tell her my parents were away, she showed up at my doorstep.

Turns out that her family was going on a mission too.

She couldn't give me any details beforehand - the typical spy routine - but it was at a Corporate Headquarters in Australia.

I was bummed that both my parents and best friend would be gone for a few days, but that's the life of a spy.

People come, and people go.

The thing that matters is whether or not they come back.

Sometimes all you need is a little faith, and trust that they can take care of themselves.

The next day following their departure was interesting.

Roy and I had been home alone without my parents many, *many* times, but this morning Roy decided to be a little... spontaneous.

It was Saturday, so I expected the typical routine of Roy working out or playing music in the living room, as he usually does when our parents were away.

Don't get me wrong, I'm usually an early bird, but no one, *no one*, beats Roy at waking up early.

But this particular Saturday morning, I woke up to the smell of something burning, and I was flying out of my bed, down the stairs, and into the kitchen in a heartbeat.

Upon my arrival in the kitchen, I found my brother covered in pancake batter, from his arms to his pants.

Flour was in his hair, and egg stained his cheek.

He was fighting with a pancake, trying to peel it off of a pan with a spatula.

The sad part was that he seemed to be losing.

I stepped forward, and he turned to face me.

"Morning, Runt." He said sheepishly.

"Um… What are you doing exactly?" I asked.

He coughed through the smoke before answering, "What does it look like? I'm making pancakes."

No sooner had he finished his sentence, the smoke alarm in our house went off.

"Or at least," he said over the beeping, "trying to."

I laughed and walked over to the counter.

I grabbed the tub of butter and a knife and walked over to the stove.

I drowned the pancake in butter to stop the sticking, and eventually the smoke detector stopped its annoying ringing.

I managed to peel the pancake off of the pan and placed it on a plate, where three other burned pancakes sat sadly.

I pointed at the charred stack.

"Those are yours." I told Roy, who was trying to clean his pants with a towel.

"How is that fair? I tried my best." He proclaimed, trying to defend himself.

"I'm sure you did." I replied, placing the pan in the sink and dousing it with hot water and soap.

Roy rolled his eyes. "This is what I get for trying."

"What were you doing making pancakes anyway? You know that cooking isn't exactly your bread and butter." I told him, letting the pan soak in the water.

Roy wiped his face with a towel before saying, "I'm expanding my horizons. I've never been good at cooking, so I figured today would be as good a day as any to try it out."

He glanced at the sad stack of burnt, rock-hard pancakes.

"I guess it didn't go so well." He said.

"Did you try to cook pancakes because you wanted to master a new skill, or because you're stressing out over Lenox and are trying to distract yourself by trying to master a new skill?" I asked.

Roy opened his mouth to protest, then shook his head. "Our sibling telepathy amazes me sometimes." He said simply.

We both smiled.

After cleaning up the kitchen and disposing of Roy's pancakes as if they were radioactive biohazards (which they might have been), my brother and I decided to head out to the local donut shop, Jerry D's Donuts, for breakfast.

The shop was calm and business was slow, as it usually was on a Saturday morning. Or, any morning really.

Most people preferred to go to Donuts Galore, the more recent and modern donut shop in town.

I'll admit, their donuts weren't bad, but no one, *no one*, beat Jerry D's.

Jerry D's wasn't just the name of the shop, it was the name of the owner.

A quiet, sweet old man, Jerry D. was 63 years old and not looking to retire any time soon.

His donuts were his pride and joy, and some days you might find some donut holes for sale when he felt spontaneous.

He baked all of his donuts himself, and if he baked too many, he gave the extra away to the younger kids who came with their parents.

Jerry was not an operative; he had no idea about any of our spy stories.

But boy, could he tell his own tales.

"So there we were, crouching behind the bush, tryin' to see what made the noise.

Then, all of a sudden, a shadow was cast in front of us.

We slowly turned to look up at a big, no, HUGE black bear, at least 11 feet tall!

He growled and slobbered, and was about to lunge at us. But oh, boy, old Roger and I knew better.

That dog and I ran for our lives away from that bush, with the bear hot at our heels! He clawed at us, and he missed me by 2 centimeters.

Roger barked at him, and I yelled to just run faster.

We managed to escape the monster, but I've learned my lesson. Never let your marshmallow roll away while you're wading in a stream barefoot." Jerry finished his story as he served Roy and I each another donut, mine chocolate and Roy's glazed.

"Wow, Jerry." Roy told him, "I bet that was *terrifying*."

"You're darn right, it was! Barely escaped with my life." Jerry replied.

I smiled and took a bite of my donut.

"Tell us another one, Jerry D. We love your stories." I said between bites of my donut.

I was being 100% honest.

Whether they were exaggerated or not, I loved hearing his tales of his normal life, with a little bit of danger thrown in.

Don't get me wrong, hearing my parents' spy stories was thrilling; but there's something about the civilian stories that gets me hooked.

"Oh, come on, now. I'm sure you kids don't want to hear another one of my boring tales." Jerry said, wiping down the counter.

"Are you kidding? Like the Runt said, we love them! Tell us one about your trip to Timbuktu." Roy told him. He loved those stories just as much as I did.

"Alright, if ya'll insist. So, I was in the savannah..." Jerry started another one of his tales.

Roy and I listened attentively, visualizing the scenarios as Jerry spoke.

Jerry was about to get to the good part, when the old phone

next to the cash register rang.

"Ugh!!" Roy and I both exclaimed when the ringer went off.

We knew Jerry would have to stop story time to answer it.

"Oh, don't whine. I'll finish in a bit." Jerry told us assuringly.

He walked to the phone and answered it, saying, "Jerry D's. And no, the 'D' doesn't stand for 'Donut'…"

Roy leaned back in his chair, wiping his mouth with his napkin. "How do you think the story will end?" He asked.

I shrugged, folding my napkin up. "With Jerry, you never know, and alien spaceship filled with unicorns could appear." I pointed out.

"True, true." Roy replied.

I was about to open my mouth to say something when Roy's phone rang.

He put his napkin down and reached in his pocket to pull his phone out.

Once he had it in front of him, I saw his facial expression change the slightest bit.

Our sibling telepathy helped me notice his face change; I knew it was O.U.O calling.

Roy gave me a look before answering, "Hello? Yup, it's me… Nothing, just getting some donuts… Yeah, she's with me, too. We're both up for a few more donuts, actually… That sounds good. Yeah, I'll be sure to let her know too… Awesome, we won't be late. Talk to ya later. Alright, bye."

Roy hung up, and I knew he had just had a conversation with Agent Amanda Carr, the woman in charge of issuing us younger operatives our missions.

Just by hearing his end of the line, I knew that Amanda had asked Roy if he was in public before asking Roy if he and I were down for a mission. Once Roy discreetly said yes, Amanda gave us our mission and said bye.

I knew how the answering-a-spy-call-in-public routine worked.

Once his phone was back in his pocket, Roy looked me right in the eye and asked, "Ready to go have some fun?"

I smiled and replied, "What do you think?"

Roy grinned and turned towards Jerry, who was wrapping up his phone call.

"Yeah, alright. Have a good day. Bye-bye." Jerry said into the receiver.

He hung up the phone and strode on over to us.

Roy looked genuinely disappointed to tell Jerry the news.

"Sorry Jerry, I just got a call. We *really* want to hear the rest of your story, but we gotta go." Roy told him.

I gave an apologetic look to Jerry before asking, "Can we hear the rest next time?"

Jerry replied, "Sure. You kids go run along. I've already told ya like 4 of my tales. One being cut off won't hurt me none."

I smiled and thanked him for the breakfast while I gathered up napkins Roy and I had used.

I set off to throw them away, and Roy took his wallet out of his pocket.

Jerry held up his hand.

"No, sir-ee, those donuts were on the house." Jerry rejected Roy's money.

Roy cocked his head and held the money out anyway.

"Come on, Jerry. Actually *take* my money for once." Roy protested.

Jerry shook his head.

"You kids and your parents are too good to me. You come in at least once a week every week and help clean and serve, ya'll never forget my birthday or the shop's anniversary, I always get a nice Christmas present from you guys, and you always, *always*, listen to my stories. NO charge today." Jerry said assertively.

Roy and I shared a look, and Roy reluctantly put his wallet away.

As Jerry passed Roy to get to the counter, he swatted him on the shoulder with his dish rag.

"Respect you're elders and know by now that there is no charge for you kids." Jerry said.

I laughed and said, "Oh, we know by now. But that doesn't

mean we won't try."

Jerry shook his head at us.

"You kids run along." He ordered.

"Yes sir, thanks a bunch." Roy and I said in unison as we walked out the door.

I slipped into the passenger seat of my brother's car and waited for Roy to take his place at the driver's seat.

Once he had closed his door, I asked, "So, what's our mission?"

"Well, Eager McBeaver," Roy said while turning the ignition, "we are going to another museum for a stake out."

"Ooh," I replied, fastening my seatbelt, "what's the loot?"

"A rare diamond from the Geraldi Museum in Monaco has received an ominous warning that it is going to be stolen very, very soon." He replied.

"Nice." I said.

We drove home, Roy called my school, we packed up for the trip, enabled the backup home security system, and were on a plane to Monaco all within 3 hours.

Needless to say, things were going to get interesting.

Chapter Eleven

"That's your fourth cup of hot chocolate." Roy pointed out.

"That's your fifth biscuit." I countered.

"Touché." Roy replied, taking another bite of his pastry.

We were both sitting inside of a café facing the Geraldi Museum, each of us partaking in the local food and drink options.

We were on a stake out, observing the museum through the huge front café windows and keeping watch for any potential thieves.

Word on the spy street had it that the museum had received an anonymous call, saying that the diamond was in serious danger, and that they needed to up security.

The heads of security at the Geraldi weren't sure what to make of the call, but my brother and I were called in to check if there was anything suspicious.

I sipped my hot chocolate as I surveyed the scene.

Several people went in and out of the museum, but I couldn't pick up any type of pattern.

It was just the normal hustle and bustle of the Geraldi.

The security cameras outside of the museum seemed to be on a constant sweeping interval, with 360 degree viewing angles.

The camera had absolutely no blind spots... at least, none non-spies could detect (when executed properly, there were 5 that could potentially be effective for evading their sight).

Roy was watching the museum too, but he had a laptop open

in front of him.

To anyone passing by, the laptop screen must have looked like it was displaying some sort of report, like something a college student would be working on.

But in reality, he was reviewing the museum security logs and security employee list.

"Stake outs always take forever." Roy pointed out in a low voice before taking another bite of his biscuit.

"Yeah… But the end result is usually satisfying." I replied, taking another swig of my hot chocolate.

I continued to watch as people passed by, one by one, on their phones, carrying bags, in conversation, in a hurry, distracted, and everything in between.

They were all living their normal lives, in their normal ways, *normally*.

The constant buzz of French speakers around me reminded me that I was a long way from home, but that's what made this mission all the more exciting.

Despite that, nothing out of the ordinary stood out to me, so I was about to turn to talk to Roy, when I saw him.

Oh, when I saw him.

I stopped short.

I almost didn't believe it when I saw Hazel Eyes, clad in his leather jacket, walk through the café doors.

He was walking up to the front counter, when he saw me out of the corner of his eye.

He stopped mid step, and smiled my way.

I smiled back, and Hazel Eyes kept walking up to the counter.

He ordered something in perfect French and stayed sitting on a stool by the counter, and he turned slightly to glance at me.

I had the urge to get up and talk to him, and I immediately felt idiotic.

Here I was, on another mission, getting distracted by the same boy.

I couldn't keep getting sidetracked this way; it just wasn't the right thing to do.

I guess Roy sensed my internal conflict, because he glanced up from his laptop screen and looked at me.

"Isn't that the guy you were talking to at the Senatru museum? What's he doing here?" Roy asked.

"I'm not sure…" I trailed off, unsure of what to say next.

"Kind of odd that he shows up at both of our ops." Roy pointed out.

It was odd. Maybe if Hazel Eyes really was connected to my missions somehow, talking would help me sort some things out.

After all, I was striking up a conversation for the sake of my mission.

"You're right, it is. Maybe I should see if I can get anything out of him." I offered.

Roy nodded, but he seemed hesitant.

I got up and walked to the counter before Roy could change his mind.

Hazel Eyes was leaning against the counter, and he glanced my way as I took the stool next to him.

"I'm sorry, do I know you from somewhere?" He asked in English.

I smiled and replied, "I'm not sure, *do* you?" in flawless French.

Hazel Eyes smiled and turned my way.

"Nice to see you, Delilah. When I said 'Don't forget me', this isn't exactly what I had in mind." He responded in French.

I raised an eyebrow. "So, what, you're not happy to see me?" I teased.

"Happy is a relative term," he replied, before turning to look back at where I had been sitting.

"Your brother's here with you, I see," he said.

I nodded, "Yeah, we're kind of a team."

Hazel Eyes smiled, saying, "I can see that."

I cocked my head, then asked, "So… What brings you here?"

Hazel Eyes smirked and replied, "I could ask you the same thing."

"Well…" I started, then trailed off, "Hazel Eyes, I asked you first."

Hazel Eyes laughed at my nickname for him, smiling, hazel eyes twinkling.

"Hazel Eyes… I like it." He said.

I smiled back at him, and waited for him to say something.

When he noticed I wasn't saying anything, he asked, "What?"

"You never answered my question. What brings you here, Hazel Eyes?" I asked.

He leaned forward, resting his elbows on the counter.

"A friend told me about the crepes that they sell here. I was in the neighborhood, so I thought I'd check them out." He said.

I didn't buy his story for a second.

He didn't look at me for a brief instance during his sentence, and he glanced down at the counter afterwards. I didn't call him out on his lie, but I did notice it.

I simply nodded, then said, "It's kind of odd that I meet you at the Senatru… then here later on."

Hazel Eyes glanced at me, then asked, "What are you saying?"

I shrugged, "You know, what are the odds?"

Hazel Eyes seemed to think for a moment before saying in English, "I'm not sure what the odds are, but I'm glad they happened."

I smiled, and I may or may not have blushed a little bit.

But I still didn't have the foggiest idea whether or not this boy had been linked to the statue being stolen, and I seriously found it unusual that I run into him twice, in the same vicinity of the same museums.

I was about to say something, when my sibling telepathy told me to glance in Roy's direction, where I saw him packing up his laptop, and he glanced at me, a 'We Gotta Get Going Like Right Now' look on his face.

I turned back to Hazel Eyes, and felt a pang of guilt for having to leave right after he said something sweet like that.

I opened my mouth to say something, when Hazel Eyes cut me off.

"Let me guess, you have to go?" He asked.

I nodded, then said, "I'm really sorry."

Hazel Eyes shook his head, "Don't be. I know the drill."

I smiled gratefully, and hopped off of my stool.

"Don't forget me." Hazel Eyes warned with a smile.

I laughed, "Why, I couldn't possibly."

Hazel Eyes smiled fondly.

I glanced at him, then said, "You know, I never got your name."

He smirked before replying, "I think nicknames are fine for now."

"Fair enough." I said.

I walked away from my mystery boy and met up with my brother at our table; Roy was putting his wallet away, and he handed me our receipt.

"Souvenir," I said simply, before slipping it into my pocket.

"Exactly." He replied, "Now, pick up your backpack and chocolate. I'll tell you the rest outside."

Chapter Twelve

L et me take a moment to declare one simple, irrefutable fact. My brother is an excellent detective.

Just by reading through the security records, he was able to deduce that one employee in particular had been taking way too many personal days, including the day that the museum had received that threatening phone call.

The security guard's name was Jared Donfrey, a 20-year-old rookie who had only been employed at the museum for 2 months.

How he was able to attain that job is beyond me.

Roy was able to pull up an employee ID photo, which I planned to cross reference with 75% of the security camera databases in the vicinity.

Roy explained to me his reasoning and I explained to him my plan.

Together, we went from the café to the museum, performing a few counter surveillance tactics along the way.

Once we walked into the Geraldi Museum, we asked to meet with the head of security, known as Mr. G.

From there, we met with Mr. G in an office at the back of the museum.

Roy and Mr. G discussed Jared Donfrey's history at the museum in French while I hacked into databases trying to find out where Jared had been in the vicinity.

I was starting to get annoyed at all of the dead ends my algorithms brought about, and Roy pointed it out by saying simply,

"Lip bite."

I bit my lip even more at his assertion.

Jared's ID photo depicted him in his security uniform, a smooth smile rested on his face. His skin was of the slightly darker variety, with dimples and deep brown eyes; his hair was brown with the slightest traces of blonde.

For a moment, just a moment, he reminded me of Hazel Eyes.

No, I thought to myself, *stop getting distracted.*

I quickly dismissed the thought and got back to work.

Mr. G explained to us that Jared, "had always been a good kid, obeyed orders in the most obedient fashion, and never showed any particular interest in the diamond."

Even with Mr. G's claims, it still seemed odd that Jared had spent only 2 months at work, yet have so many personal days taken.

"Well, it seems to me that Jared had spent more time *out* of work than actually *in* work." I pointed out to Mr. G.

Mr. G shook his head, and replied, "That's a matter of opinion."

I could see it in his eyes that he really wanted to give Jared the benefit of the doubt; that he was innocent and this was all a huge coincidence.

But I could also tell that Mr. G was slowly starting to see things from our point of view.

And he didn't like what we thought.

Mr. G excused himself and exited the office, leaving Roy and I alone.

"He doesn't believe us." Roy said in English.

"He doesn't *want* to believe us." I countered.

"Whatever," he replied, waving his hand at me, "we just need some proof to back us up. Do you have anything yet?"

"Just... one... minute..." I replied, checking security footage left and right.

"Well, have you checked all of the cafés?" He asked.

"Yes." I replied.

"Grocery stores?"

"Yes."

"Restaurants?"

"Yes."

"Movies?"

"Yes."

"Churches?"

"*Yes.*"

"Those cameras they have at stop lights when you run a red light?"

"That was the *first* place I checked."

Roy sighed, saying, "There has to be at least *one* place where he's been."

"Well, I... GOT IT!" I exclaimed.

Roy came up behind me to look at my work on the laptop.

"See? The security cameras at a hotel caught him leaving his room 2 hours ago, real time." I told him.

Roy grinned and clapped me on the back. "Nice job, Runt. What are we waiting for?"

I smiled and said, "Let's go."

The hotel was a skyscraper, shooting off into the expanse of blue above me.

I wasn't used to the big, crowded city life, but it didn't faze me enough to be so astounded I couldn't move.

Roy on the other hand, just waltzed up to the building.

"Wait, what are you doing?" I asked him.

Roy looked at me is if it were obvious.

"You know, you can't just waltz through the front doors of a hotel in a foreign country and ask for a man you haven't even met!" I pointed out.

Roy raised an eyebrow, "Who said anything about the front doors?"

It finally clicked in my head what he had in mind, and I have to admit, I kind of loved it.

Silently, we made our way to the back of the building, dodging security cameras and avoiding security guards.

Once we were out of sight at the back of the hotel, we needed to find a way to get to the third balcony; that was where Jared's room was.

Roy used his binoculars to check out the two balconies we were going to have to pass in order to get to the third one, and thankfully he gave me the all clear.

"It's our lucky day, there's no one home on the first balcony, and the curtains are closed on the second." He said.

He turned to me and asked, "Did you bring the gear?"

I pulled a rope and grappling hook out of my back pack, and I pushed a button on the hook to make it expand from a skinny stick to a curved, three branched piece of spy equipment.

"Of course," I replied, swinging the rope in a circle, in an attempt to gain momentum.

Once I figured I had enough speed, I tossed it up, and I managed to hook it onto the first balcony.

"Nice. You go first," Roy told me, turning this way and that, trying to see if anyone spotted us.

I grabbed onto the rope and hugged it with my knees.

From there I began to climb up, anxious to get to the third balcony.

Once I had made it to the first balcony, I threw my arms over to steady myself, pulled myself up, and swung my legs over.

I landed safely and softly on the balcony floor.

I leaned over to see Roy already on his way up, and once he reached me I helped him over the balcony's side.

"One down." Roy said.

"Two to go." I replied.

Once we had repeated the process the remaining two times, we found ourselves outside of Jared's balcony window, and I was already at work picking the lock.

"You did run a loop on the security cameras on this side of the building so that we wouldn't be seen, right?" Roy asked.

I faked being offended as I responded, "Of course, what do you take me for, a Level 1 Clearance Operative?"

Roy laughed and flicked me on my shoulder.

"Just hurry up with the lock." He said.

Once I had finished, Roy and I were in Jared's room and doing some snooping around.

We both had on our flat soled shoes so as not to leave any telltale foot prints, and gloves to match.

"You'd think for a 20 -year-old living on his own this guy would be a little… well… *messy*." I pointed out.

Roy inspected a bag of clothes as he replied, "Not all men are messy, thank you Ms. Stereotype."

"That's not what I mean. Look around, *nothing* is out of place, the bed is made, all of his clothes are ironed and hung… even the trash is crushed and placed neatly in the can!" I said incredulously.

Roy started to ponder my point of view.

"Maybe he's a neat freak who gets sick a lot, that's why he's been missing work so much." Roy voiced his idea, although I knew he didn't believe it.

"It's weird how he doesn't have any pictures up. None of himself, family, friends, nothing." I said.

"Aren't you just the clever little observer. It's a *hotel room*." Roy teased, crouching down to peek underneath the bed.

"Still. He's been living here for a while, I would have thought he would have *something* up." I defended myself.

"Everybody's different." Roy pointed out.

I sighed. "I just hope we find something that proves he's guilty, or else we're just two spies going through a random stranger's hotel room."

"Well, does *this* prove anything?" Roy asked, pulling an old, beat up black notebook out from under the mattress.

I bounded over to take a look, and we flipped through the pages.

All previous pages had been ripped out, so that there was just a thick layer of paper where the sheets had been ripped away from.

There were still pages left in the book, but the only one with anything on it had a sketch of the diamond at the Geraldi museum, with "Monaco" written underneath in pencil.

There was also a big red 'X' on the drawing, with a caption that read, "Target cannot be obtained. Thank little bro."

I glanced at Roy, who had the same puzzled expression as I did.

"So, Jared's *not* going after the diamond after all." I said.

Roy nodded, "We have his 'little bro' to thank for that."

I held my HoloWatch up to the notebook and snapped a few pictures.

This was the proof Roy and I needed to convince Mr. G that Jared was guilty.

"Did you find anything else?" Roy asked.

I shook my head. "The rest of this place is clean." I replied.

"Well, we better get going. Jared can walk in at any minute." Roy said.

As if on cue, we heard foot steps outside the door in the hallway.

"Good afternoon, Mr. Donfrey!" An elderly female voice said in broken English.

"Afternoon, Mrs. Louise." A male voice replied.

Roy and I looked at each other with an, 'Oh My Goodness Gracious' expression, and quickly made our way to the balcony.

Roy put the notebook back exactly the way he had found it, and he made sure to check that everything was exactly as it had been before we had broken in.

We rushed out the window, and I locked it behind me, triple checking that there was no evidence that it had been tampered with.

I turned towards Roy to see that he had already set the rope and hook back up, and was checking to make sure that the bottom two hotel rooms were still empty.

Roy looked at me and gave the all clear, to which I then started making my way down the rope to the second story balcony.

Roy followed behind me, and in a matter of minutes we were back on solid ground, and on our way back to the museum to bust our perp.

Seeing the look on Mr. G's face as we showed him the pictures broke my heart.

Mr. G really had his heart set on Jared being innocent, and the notebook we found absolutely shattered that theory.

Once Mr. G had agreed that we needed to apprehend Jared and that the security had to be reinforced around the diamond, we were on our way back to Jared's hotel room to place him under arrest.

We totally didn't expect what came next: Jared was gone; left without a trace.

The clerk at the front desk claimed that Jared had checked out half an hour ago, completely packed up with all of his belongings.

Mr. G asked permission to search his room, with the excuse that it was a matter of extreme museum-related importance.

The clerk was hesitant, but he gave his consent.

Mr. G went in with Roy to search Jared's room while I kept watch in the lobby, in case I caught sight of Jared or anything involving him.

"I'm on comms if you need me. Just wait here." Roy told me before walking off with Mr. G.

Next thing I know, a particularly cute and familiar boy was walking into the hotel, with a backpack slung over his shoulder.

I couldn't believe it.

Hazel Eyes had a seriously irritable look on his face, and he practically fell into a chair by the front doors.

He gave a huge sigh and ran a hand through his hair be-fore rubbing his eyes in what seemed to be a mix of fatigue and frustration.

He hadn't seen me yet, and I wasn't sure whether or not I should make myself known.

I glanced around the lobby and came to the conclusion that

Jared was probably long gone, after all, why would he return to the place he just left?

I walked over to Hazel Eyes, and sat in the chair next to him.

He had his face in his hands, and glanced over at me.

When he realized it was me, he smiled and lifted his head.

"Hey there, Delilah. Are you following me?" He asked.

"I should be asking you that question." I countered.

He laughed and leaned back in his chair, the frustration in his face gone, replaced with his normal composure.

"What brings you here?" He asked.

I had to think fast; I totally hadn't been expecting him to show up here.

Luckily, I was trained to think on my feet.

But his hazel eyes weren't making it easy for me to lie.

"I'm staying here with my brother. He's double checking that we didn't leave anything in our room." I replied.

Not the best lie I've ever told, but he seemed to believe it.

Hazel Eyes nodded at me, but didn't say anything else.

I gave him a suspicious look.

"What?" He asked, feigning innocence.

"Aren't you going to tell me what *you're* doing here?" I asked.

Hazel Eyes smirked and said, "I was supposed to meet someone here, but they never showed. Now I'm stuck here until I think of some way to find them."

I would have believed that he was lying, but there was something in his voice that seemed genuine.

He was telling the truth.

"Anything I can do to help?" I offered.

"It's complicated. I don't think you could do much." He replied.

He must have seen the look on my face, because he quickly recovered, saying, "Not that I don't think you're not capable, it's just… complicated."

I nodded and said, "I like complicated."

He looked at me and said, "Well, you'd be the first."

"There's a first time for everything." I said optimistically.

"There is, isn't there?" He replied.

Before I could respond, I heard my brother's voice in my ear, telling me that he and Mr. G were on their way back to the lobby.

Once again, I had let myself get distracted by Hazel Eyes and his... well... *hazel eyes.*

I rose from my seat, and Hazel Eyes looked up at me.

"You're going to leave without saying goodbye?" He asked sarcastically.

I laughed and said, "I've seen you so much lately, what are the chances that this is goodbye?"

"That's true," he said, leaning back in his chair and looking up at me, in such a way that it was almost as if he were admiring me with those hazel eyes of his.

"I'll see you around. Don't forget me." He said.

I smiled, and replied, "You know I won't."

I walked away just as Roy and Mr. G entered the lobby.

"Did you find anything?" I asked them.

Roy shook his head, saying, "The place is clean. He's gone."

I gave Mr. G a sympathetic look, and we headed out.

All three of us walked out of the hotel nonchalantly, as if we walked in and out of that place on a daily basis.

Hazel Eyes watched us leave, but instead of a smile, he looked perplexed.

I just walked away.

Chapter Thirteen

*O*nce Roy and I had tied up all of our loose ends back at the Geraldi Museum, we packed up and headed home.

Both Scarlet's family and my parents had returned while Roy and I were gone, and I was so glad to see them.

There's nothing like coming home from a mission and having a fresh grilled cheese sandwich made by your parents waiting for you.

My mom seemed especially glad to see me, and I worried that her special mom intuition would have led her to notice my recent distracted states, all caused by Hazel Eyes.

But she never said a word, and I didn't either.

My least favorite thing about coming home after a mission was the pile of homework that greeted me when I came back.

If you think missing work at a regular school is tough, try missing work at a spy school.

It's a million times worse.

Mr. Needlemeyer had assigned a packet that was 75 pages thick, double sided.

I was pretty sure it would take me half a lifetime to get it done.

My Covert Field Research Course teacher, Miss Kidman, had shown slightly less mercy by assigning us the task of tailing a police officer and getting an imprint of his squad car keys.

I'm sure that was going to be easy.

I had several other assignments, including, but not limited to, learning 45 new vocabulary words in Farsi and Latin *each*, writing a 10 page report on the impracticality of our government's Secret Service gadgets, and finding 10 valid reasons on why John Donne was actually an English spy.

I was going to have a fun night.

As I picked up my pen to get started, my mind drifted back to Monaco, thinking about Hazel Eyes and our odd encounters.

Why had we run into each other so much?

Could his appearances and my missions be connected somehow?

What was he thinking when he leaned back and looked at me like that in the lobby?

Why was I focusing on these questions when I had a mountain of school-related questions I needed to tackle?

I decided to snap myself out of my girly daydreaming faze and get started.

After hours of work, only two five minute breaks, and a quick run to the police station, my head finally hit my pillow at 5:00 am, and my alarm went off at 6:30.

Such is the life of a sophomore spy kid at Henderson High.

Once I had tamed my hair, brushed my teeth, picked out an outfit, greeted my family, eaten breakfast, double checked I had everything for school, said bye to my family and headed out the door, it was 7:15 am, and I was looking forward to getting back into my school routine.

I walked over to Scarlet's house on my way to school, and she was putting on lip gloss as she shut her front door behind her.

"Really?" I asked as she met me at the end of her driveway.

She glared at me and said, "You of all people should know that multi-tasking is not just a skill, it's an art."

I laughed and rolled my eyes as we started walking.

"Whatever you say." I replied.

"Anything exciting happen on your mission?" She asked, genuinely curious.

I smiled and said, "Actually, yeah. I ran into Hazel Eyes again, *twice*. He seemed happy to see me, but I can't help but wonder why I keep seeing him so often."

Scarlet smiled her mischievous, gossipy smile and replied, "Maybe it's fate that you two keep meeting each other. Maybe you're both destined to be caught up in something huge later on."

I thought over what she said before saying, "Maybe. I don't know. All I know is that he keeps popping up during my missions, and I keep getting distracted."

Scarlet looked at me in the way only a best friend can, and said, "Maybe you should stop calling them 'distractions' and see them as opportunities."

"Yeah, opportunities to get distracted." I countered.

Scarlet shook her head, "Sometimes you're just impossible, you know that?"

I smiled and replied, "You know you love me."

Scarlet laughed and I asked her, "So, how did your mission go?"

"Well, it didn't have a cute mystery boy in it, but I did end up stuck in an elevator for 2 hours, so that was fun." She said.

I laughed and gave her a quizzical look.

She held up a hand as she said, "Don't ask."

"Alright." I said compliantly.

"So, did you finish the packet for Needlemeyer?" She asked me.

"Surprisingly, yes. Just ask the bags under my eyes." I replied.

Scarlet laughed and said, "I finished too. In fact, I got everything done except for that John Donne assignment. I still need one piece of evidence."

"He wrote about not asking for whom the bell tolls, obviously the bell was just a code name for some sort of op he was on." I said.

Scarlet cocked her head and pondered my statement.

"This is why you get A's in every class, isn't it?" She asked.

I laughed as we walked onto campus.

We headed over to our lockers, and as I slipped my AP World History book, *The History of Everything: The Extended Version*, into my locker, James Peters walked up.

"Hey, Kay." He greeted me with a smile.

"Hey, James. What's up?" I asked.

James leaned against the lockers and said, "Well, since you've missed 2 days of PE, I was wondering if you might need someone to help catch you up on what we've been up to."

I glanced at Scarlet, who made an 'Aw He's Trying To Be Cute' face back at me.

"Um, sure James. It wouldn't hurt to be caught up. What did you have in mind?" I asked.

James seemed to think for a bit before responding, "What about during lunch? Once you're done eating I'll come by and we can practice in the gym. You know Coach doesn't mind."

As much as I appreciated his effort to be friendly, I wasn't sure if I really wanted to spend half of my lunch time with James working on soccer moves.

Scarlet gave me a subtle thumbs up before closing her locker, signaling that I should accept.

I turned to James and said, "You know what? That sounds good. Thanks for offering, James."

He smiled and replied, "See you later," before walking away.

Scarlet watched as James walked away, and once he was out of earshot, she said, "He didn't even say hi to me. Did you notice that?"

I nodded before replying, "You know how rude he can be. I'm just a little surprised he would be so nice like that."

"Maybe he likes you." Scarlet pointed out.

I rolled my eyes, "You just have to bring up crushes, don't you?" I asked, smiling.

Scarlet raised her hands up in surrender, saying, "It's a valid point."

I laughed as I closed my locker, and we both walked to our usual spot in Miss Kidman's classroom as we waited for the school day to start.

Miss Kidman was one of my favorite teachers, and Scarlet and I always hung out in her room when class wasn't in session.

Miss Kidman didn't mind, in fact, she welcomed it.

Miss K was about 25 years old, and she was the youngest

teacher at Henderson; everyone loved her "hip" personality.

"Did you hear about the eighth grader who almost walked into Mr. Fitzgerald's room while he and the class were experimenting with an invisibility serum? Ooh, it was a close call. Luckily, a student saw him coming from the one way glass window on the door and ran to lock the door before he could get in." Miss Kidman told us the stories of what had happened while Scarlet and I were away.

"That's insane. All of the spy kids know that the last one in the room locks the door." I pointed out.

"I know. Eighth graders." Scarlet said, shaking her head.

"I remember when we were in eighth grade. Intro to AP Economics and Pre-AP Biology. Those were the days." Scarlet said wistfully.

Miss Kidman laughed and said, "Oh, come on. You kids don't have half as much work as us teachers. Sure, you have to do all of the assignments, but we have to *grade*... Every. Single. One. Would you want to trade?"

I smiled and shook my head, but Scarlet wasn't going to get off the subject without her getting her own input in.

"You know, if teachers assigned *us* less work, then that would equal less work for *you*..." She trailed off.

Miss Kidman raised an eyebrow, saying, "Scarlet, I am not going to propose cutting down the homework and assignments we give to you students at the next staff meeting. It's just not happening."

Scarlet pouted. "It was worth a try."

I laughed and glanced at the clock on Miss Kidman's desk.

My internal clock was telling me that it was 8:15 am, and her clock verified my thoughts.

We still had 15 minutes before class began, so we stayed in Miss Kidman's room a while longer.

"By the way, is the squad car key imprint assignment due in class?" I asked.

Miss Kidman nodded before taking a swig of coffee from her bright orange mug.

"It's due, not today, but *next* class period. I had some students complaining about the time frame." Miss Kidman informed us, with an eye roll.

"That's ridiculous. We go to *spy* school. What do they expect?" I voiced my opinion.

Miss Kidman nodded in agreement.

Scarlet turned to look at me before saying, "You have no idea how hard it is to distract a police officer long enough to swipe their keys *and* put them back."

"Actually, yeah, I do. Remember the Brooklyn Op?" I asked her.

"Ohhh, yeah! Man, that was a good mission." She said with a smile.

"I did the same thing, except I asked for an interview for a school assignment, so it wasn't necessarily a hasty distraction." I said.

"Oh, you girls." Miss Kidman said, smiling.

We stayed talking in her room until the bell rang, and from there Scarlet and I set off for our first period class.

We sat through our Dialects and Calligraphy of the World class, then we went our separate ways as she went to AP World History and I went to Advanced Calculus.

Soon enough, lunch time rolled around, and I found myself finishing my food underneath a tree with Scarlet next to me.

"Hmm, looks like someone's almost done with her pizza... Could it be that it's James Peters time?" She asked between bites of her burger.

I rolled my eyes with a smile before taking the final bite of my cheese pizza.

A few minutes later, James walked up to the tree and smiled down at me.

"Ready, to practice, Kay?" he asked.

I stood up, saying, "Yeah, just let me pack up."

"Alright. Hey, Scarlet." James said.

Scarlet held a hand to her heart and faked shock, saying, "He acknowledged my presence. My life is complete."

I laughed, then quickly stopped myself when I saw James's face.

"Well, I'll go find Ted and talk about the Chemistry homework while you two go do your thing." Scarlet planned.

I gave her a sideways glance, saying, "Talk to Ted about the 'Chemistry Assignment', huh? You couldn't go chat with Sandra, or Leah, or Julian? They're in our class too."

Scarlet slung her backpack over her shoulder before replying, "I have a question about... mole conversion."

"Uh, huh." I replied, picking up my own backpack and trying to hide my smile.

"Just go with James." She said irritably.

"Alright, Miss Crabby. See you later." I told her, laughing.

"See you, Miss Nosy." She replied, smiling.

James and I walked to the gym, chatting about normal school things, and once we got to the gym, James headed straight for the bleachers and sat down.

There wasn't a soccer ball in sight, so I grew a little suspicious as I took my backpack off.

"This isn't really about practicing soccer moves, I have an important question I need to ask you. Go ahead and sit." He said, setting his own backpack next to him.

"Okay... What's up?" I asked, sitting next to him.

He took a deep breath before starting, "So, there's this gala next Saturday in Houston, and... as much as it pains me to say this... I-I- need your help."

My curiosity peaked as I looked at James and asked, "What kind of help?"

He rubbed his hands together before saying, "There's going to be countless rich folk, and you know where there's a pretty penny..."

"There are thieves waiting to pick it up." I finished for him.

James nodded, "Exactly. My parents have been hunting down a particularly elusive art thief, and we have reason to believe that he'll be there at the gala. I just... Um, wanted you to help me find him. I want to show my parents what I'm really capable of, and I figured I could use your help. Plus, they told me that I could invite one person, and their family could tag along. I just… I need your help."

I smiled, touched that James had humbled himself enough to willingly ask for help.

I opened my mouth to say so, when James continued talking.

"Of course, I can handle this on my own, no problem. I just thought an extra hand could be… useful. And anyway, if we do catch him, my parents would be proud of my handiwork." He finished.

"*Your* handiwork?" I asked.

James clasped his hands together before saying, "Will you help me or not?"

I pondered his offer for a moment, weighing what James was asking of me.

He wanted me and my whole family to drop everything and head to Houston this coming Saturday to help catch an art thief.

Such is the life of a spy.

"I'll have to ask my parents, but as for me, my answer is yes." I replied.

James smiled before rising to his feet.

"Alright then. I hope to see you there." He said.

James picked up his backpack and headed out of the gym, leaving me at the bleachers.

My internal clock told me that I had about 10 minutes left before CFRC, so I set out to find Scarlet.

I found her chatting with Ted, and they seemed to be deep in conversation.

"Hey, guys." I said as I walked up.

"Oh, hey, Kay. Finished with James so soon?" Scarlet asked.

"Yeah, we wrapped up pretty quickly. Thought I'd come find you." I replied.

"Well, Scarlet and I were just talking about Mr. Needlemeyer and the crazy amount of homework he gives out." Ted said with a smile.

"Oh, he sure does, doesn't he?" I asked, with a bright smile towards Scarlet.

Scarlet gave a nervous, yet genuine smile back as she said, "Yeah, he does."

We talked a little while more and headed for class once the bell rang.

On the way to class, I told Scarlet what James really wanted, and she mischievously replied how interesting it all was.

Chapter Fourteen

*A*s we took our usual seats in Miss Kidman's classroom, I noticed that on her whiteboard she had taped three pictures, each depicting the same man in 3 different places.

I glanced at Scarlet, and she was looking at the pictures too.

We exchanged a glance, and patiently waited for class to start to see what the 3 pictures had to do with anything.

Miss Kidman walked out of a closet with a small cardboard box, her boots silent as she stepped across the room.

"Past, present, future. Where, when, why. Bacon, lettuce, tomato. Me, myself, I. Should have, would have, could have. The majority of things in life come in threes. Why this is so, nobody can say for sure. But what we do know, is that 3 is a magic number in our profession." Miss Kidman began her lecture as she walked to her desk and set the box down.

"Does anybody know *why* 3 is such a significant number in an operative's life?" She asked, opening the box.

A girl named Jessie raised her hand, and when Miss Kidman called on her, she said, "Three tools during an op will ensure success?"

"A good guess, but no. Anyone else?" Miss Kidman asked.

A hand that belonged to a boy named Mark rose, and once he was called on, he voiced his guess, "When you get the same intel from three sources, you know it's credible."

"Mm, not quite. But you're on the right track." Miss Kidman encouraged.

I raised my own hand, and after I was called on, I said, "When you meet someone, or run into something, *three* times, that's when you know there's something more to it."

Miss Kidman pointed at me with her index finger and said simply, "Bingo."

She walked over to the whiteboard, and pointed at the first picture of the man.

He was wearing a dark hat, a leather jacket, and had slight stubble on his chin.

He looked completely ordinary.

"If you saw this man during an op walking down the street at the same time you were, would you think anything of him? Be honest." Miss Kidman looked out towards us.

The entire class shook their heads.

She walked a little down the line until she was pointing at the second picture.

This time, the man was in a white t-shirt, with sunglasses sitting on top of his head. His stubble was gone.

"If you saw this man a second time, also during an op, walking down the street at the same time you were in a completely different location, would you think anything of him then? Be honest." Miss Kidman warned.

Half of the class nodded while the other half pondered it for a moment.

I nodded.

Finally, Miss Kidman walked over to the third picture, where the man was wearing a tuxedo and was adjusting his cuff links.

Miss Kidman pointed to the picture and asked again, "If you saw this man for a third time, also during an op, walking down the street at the same time you were in *another* completely different location, would you think anything of him? Be honest."

The entire class nodded.

"They say that 'third time's the charm', but I beg to differ. No, the third time means that there's something more to what you have in front of you; something big is coming. Whether it be good or bad, you'll never know until it happens. Pay attention to the things that happen not only *to* you, but also *around* you, so that maybe you'll notice things from a different perspective." She lectured us as she pulled out a snow globe, a chew toy, and a red high heel from the box.

"I want you all to list 3 situations where each of these items can lead to scenarios that you would never think of just by glancing at them. Be creative, and remember, in this business, anything can happen." She told us our assignment as she arranged the three objects in a line on her desk.

The whole class began the assignment, some starting with the snow globe and ending with the heel, other skipping around, jotting down whatever popped into their heads.

Once everyone had finished, we each voiced one idea per item; I have to admit, some were pretty out there.

One boy conspired that the snow globe was actually a transport device that held a rare liquid that replaces water and was being transported to be duplicated.

Scarlet claimed that the chew toy contained a tracking device that was activated when pressure was applied, and it was used to track thieves who loved their animal companions.

I said that the high heel was actually a device that left so called "bread crumbs" with every step it took; special infrared technology would track a certain footprint left by the heel, and operatives could track whomever was wearing the shoe.

Miss Kidman enjoyed hearing our theories, and even added her own spin to them when she deemed it appropriate.

By the time every student had gone, there was approximately 3.27 minutes of class left.

"So, I hope you all have come to realize that often there is more than meets the eye. Be vigilant in your observance skills, and once something makes itself known a *third* time, something serious is going on. Don't just brush it aside, something obscure could be conspiring." Miss Kidman finished her lecture and began packing up her box, saying, "Pass your papers to the front, and I will collect them shortly."

As the papers filled with weird scenarios flowed to the front of each desk row, Scarlet raised her hand.

"Yes?" Miss Kidman asked, never even looking in Scarlet's direction.

"Just out of curiosity ma'am, who *is* the man in the pictures?" Scarlet asked.

"Oh, him?" Miss Kidman asked, smiling at the pictures, "that's my boyfriend."

Shortly after that, the bell rang, and the rest of my day went on.

I could hardly focus in AP Computer Sciences after that lecture; I kept thinking about Hazel Eyes.

I had run into him in two different places, and I don't know what I was going to do if I ran into him a third.

If three really was the magic number in the spy game, then what was in store for Hazel Eyes and I in the future?

Were we meant to have something good happen to us?

Or were we going to crash and burn?

My mind raced as I tried to figure things out, but after a while, I just decided to wait and see if I faced a third encounter.

After all, even if Hazel Eyes and I *were* meant for something more…

What was the worst that could happen?

Chapter Fifteen

*T*hat Saturday, I found myself putting on a dress I never thought I would wear, and attempting to walk around in heels I never thought I would use, as I was getting ready for the gala.

My parents had agreed to take a small vacation to Houston, so we left Friday night, arrived early Saturday morning, slept during the day, and were getting ready in the late afternoon.

Roy was tying a red tie around his neck while looking in the mirror, making sure his hair was gelled and combed properly.

His tuxedo was oozing fancy, and his cuff links and watch were especially dapper.

My mom looked absolutely stunning in her midnight blue gown.

It had jewels at the waist, and it cascaded gracefully to the floor, with a small slit on her left leg.

Her hair was curly and framed her face beautifully; she wore a dazzling diamond necklace with a bracelet to match.

Her makeup was flawless; not too much, not too little, and just the right amount of elegance.

My dad was in his own posh suit and tie, looking sharp and worth a million bucks (which is almost what his watch cost, since it doubled as a laser).

His blue tie set off his outfit, and his cuff links and watch matched each other.

As for me, I had on a red ball gown that sported small embellishments on the waist and in sparing, random areas on the skirt.

My hair had been swooped up into a bun, with my side bangs spinning down in curls on the sides of my face.

I had some jeweled beads in my hair here and there, adding some sparkle, with an emerald necklace and bracelet to match.

I wore the slightest traces of makeup, just to show that I *did* have makeup on.

"Are we *sure* we want her going in like that? She might draw some extra attention to herself..." Roy said in his special big-brother tone.

My dad stepped up to me and crossed his arms.

"Hm, you know son, you're right. Maybe she should put on some jeans instead. Oh, and a baggy sweatshirt. That should keep eager eyes at bay." He joked.

"Leave Kay alone, boys. She looks beautiful." My mother swooped in to save me from their ridicules as she placed her hands on my shoulders.

"She's my beautiful baby girl." My mother said wistfully, staring at both of us in the mirror.

"Yeah, well, she's my annoying baby sister. It's my job to be annoyingly overprotective." Roy pointed out.

"You certainly do a good job of it." I retorted.

Roy smiled and flicked me on the shoulder.

I smiled back.

Once we were 100% ready and packed, we headed out to the gala as a whole.

When my parents were out of earshot, Roy grabbed me by the shoulder, stopping me mid step.

I gave him a questionable look, but his face was completely serious.

He leaned down and whispered, "I know that *he* was there at the hotel. First the Senatru, then the café. What is going on with him? Do you know this guy?"

Roy gave me a stern, yet concerned look; he genuinely wanted to know.

I looked up at him, and simply whispered, "I… I don't know. He's been showing up lately at the same places we have, but I don't even know his name. I have no idea what he was doing at any of the places, but he's just a boy. I-I don't know anything about him."

The truth of my statement cut me deeply.

I really had no idea who Hazel Eyes was, I don't even know his *name.*

Yes, I enjoyed talking to him, and he seemed to like talking to me, but I had no clue who he really was.

We had only ever exchanged a few sentences, yet he was almost always on my mind.

How was that possible?

Roy simply nodded, but I could see it in his eyes that he didn't believe me completely.

I continued walking out the door, on my way to the gala and my mission to help James.

The venue was amazing.

Stunning candlelight glowed in candelabras that speckled the gala space, and they helped contribute to the classy ambiance.

Gorgeous chandeliers hung from the ceiling and sparkled in the light. Rainbow flecks twinkled off of them, mesmerizingly beautiful.

The floor was made of limestone tiles, emphasizing the fancy feel.

There were floor to ceiling pillars that were made of granite, and they spiraled up from top to bottom.

Several waiters were moving about the room, holding up silver platters in one hand with white handkerchiefs draped over an arm.

An orchestra in impeccable suits and dresses were playing classical musical in the front of the room, and the way they blended their separate instruments together was, in a word, incredible.

The people attending the gala were of the upper class, no doubt about it.

The men were all dressed in perfectly tailored suits, with ties and cuff links that were of the pricey variety.

I'm pretty sure that the price of their watches all together was worth over 12 million dollars.

The women were a completely different story.

Everywhere you looked, there were stunning ball gowns flowing on beautiful women, and the jewelry they wore had to be worth over 49 million dollars.

But there wasn't just the wealthy roaming around.

I recognized several other agents, some under the employment of O.U.O, others from the C.I.A, F.B.I, and more.

But there was also the undesirable bunch of the crowd.

I knew that thieves were among the people I saw before me, blending in with the "it" crowd, acting like the fellow common rich man.

They were in the shadows, and they acted like any other gala-goer in this venue.

It was going to be tough tracking down the art thief James was looking for.

My family and I agreed to split up while I talked to James to get intel, and then I would tell them the details through my comms unit.

Once we found the thief, we would call in James and help apprehend the art thief without causing too much commotion.

Roy went to the front of the room, while my mom and dad went to the left.

I went to the right and met up with James for a briefing.

"Wow, you clean up nice." He said, as I walked up.

"Um, thanks. You too." I replied.

James was in a navy suit with striped gray tie, and his watched matched his cuff links.

"You look good, Kay. You look… really good." James said in a way that made me think he didn't realize he was talking out loud.

I simply smiled and said, "You look good, too. Now, whom exactly are we looking for?"

James snapped out of whatever state he was in and got down to business.

"Ok. His name is Damian Quarters, light complexion, around his mid-thirties, black hair, trimmed beard, blue eyes, about 6-foot-two. He has a birthmark on his right wrist, and a scar on his left temple." James said, pulling out a small, blurry picture from his coat pocket.

I took a good look at it, memorizing every detail I discerned.

James slipped the image back into his pocket after 2 minutes, so as not to raise suspicion.

"Oh, and he likes shrimp." James added.

I gave James a questionable look as to how he knew that, and he simply responded, "Don't ask."

I nodded and said, "My family and I are on it, we're all looking for him, and I'll give them the details right now."

James nodded his approval, and before I walked away he said, "Oh, and Kay?"

I turned around to see James looking at the ground, almost too embarrassed to look me in the eye.

"Thank you for everything." He said in a small voice.

He glanced up at me, and I smiled, replying, "You're welcome."

I walked away smiling, and once I was a few feet away I blended in with a corner of the room and gave my family the details through my comms unit.

Roy said he had already been studying faces, and he would back track to see if he recognized any.

My parents were getting acquainted with several people, seeing if anyone knew Damian Quarters.

I began walking about the room, scanning faces, greeting people, making polite conversation here and there.

I was just another rich teenager in the crowd.

It surprised me how many children of the guests had come; personally, all of this fancy business wasn't my style.

But, for the sake of my mission, I was enduring it.

After walking around for a while, I decided to stop and just watch the churning crowd of elegance, and I rested by a candelabra.

I admired the details on it; the gold had brass trimmings, and several small gems were added to the base.

I noticed that one was loose, almost to the point of falling.

I took a quick glance around to see if anyone was watching, and once I was in the clear, I plucked the gem off of the base and stuck it to my spy bracelet (it had special adhesive space in the bottom to hold any small object I found without sticking to my wrist).

Without the gem, the candelabra looked exactly the same.

You literally couldn't tell that the one gem was missing.

Souvenir, I thought to myself, a smile crossing my face.

I continued surveying the crowd, watching as men danced with their wives, teenagers mingled, and waiters served food on platters.

Nothing seemed out of the ordinary for a venue like this, so I decided to start my walk about again, when I heard a voice behind me.

"Third time's the charm, isn't it, Delilah?"

I froze, in utter disbelief at what I was hearing.

I turned around to see Hazel Eyes, clad in a deep gray, almost black tuxedo, with a deep green tie.

His hair had been combed to the side, so that it wasn't in the comfortably messy, yet cute style I had previously seen.

It was still pretty darn good looking.

His face wore a smooth, easy smile, and his hazel eyes sparkled in the candlelight.

I fought my hardest to keep from swooning.

Hazel Eyes walked up to me, and when he reached me he said, "You look..." he trailed off, staring at me with those dreamy hazel eyes of his.

I would have given anything to know what he was thinking right then, the way he looked at me, smiling genuinely, yet distantly.

Finally, he spoke, "Beautiful."

I wanted to melt.

I had never been called beautiful by anyone other than my parents, Roy, or Scarlet, and I seriously considered hugging Hazel Eyes for the compliment.

I blushed and stayed silent, not knowing what to say.

Finally, I said, "I don't know about beautiful, but... Thank you. You look nice, too. So handsome."

Hazel Eyes laughed and said, "Don't lie to me, Delilah. I know I look dorky. I'm not fond of monkey suits."

It took me a while to process the fact that he thought he didn't look good; he thought he looked dorky.

"Are you kidding? I'm not fond of this type of attire either, but why would I lie about you looking handsome?" I asked.

Hazel Eyes cocked his head slightly before responding, "I wasn't saying you were lying about me looking nice. I'm saying don't lie about not knowing how beautiful you are."

I was stunned; I hadn't been expecting that kind of response.

Before I could open my mouth to speak, the severity of the situation hit me completely.

Here I was, on a mission, running into Hazel Eyes, *again*, for the *third* time in a *row*.

Here I was, on a mission, getting distracted by Hazel Eyes, *again*, for the *third* time in a *row*.

Here I was, on a mission, being called beautiful by Hazel Eyes, and being dumbfounded to the point of not knowing what to say.

What was I *doing*?!

I was on a mission to catch an art thief; James was counting on me!

I didn't even know this boy's *name*, and I was letting myself talk to him, laugh with him, get lost in him.

For the third time, I was sidetracked and confused, not knowing where Hazel Eyes fit in the larger picture.

What did he mean for me?

Hazel Eyes took a step forward, and he came close to me, closer than we had ever been in our previous encounters.

He leaned down slightly and whispered, in a concerned tone,

"I need to talk to you."

I didn't know what to do.

"I…" I started, not knowing what was going to come out of my mouth next, when I saw him.

A man, about 6-foot-two, in his mid-thirties, with black hair.

When he lifted up his jacket sleeve to check the time, a birthmark on his right wrist greeted him.

The scar on his left temple was barely visible, a vain attempt to cover it up with cheap makeup had been made.

His beard had been shaved, and his smooth, clean skin revealed an incredibly rugged jawline.

And he was eating a shrimp from a waiter's platter.

In short: standing 15 feet away in from of me, was Damian Quarters.

And Hazel Eyes was literally right in my way.

I was caught between Hazel Eyes and hearing what he had to say, and the target of my mission.

Maybe Hazel Eyes was going to give me answers, let me know *why* our two worlds kept colliding.

Damian Quarters was standing just a stone's throw away, easily within reach.

If I talked with Hazel Eyes, maybe my questions would be answered, I wouldn't be so distracted anymore, and Damian would still be at the gala to capture later.

But there was the possibility that Damian would leave, or I would lose him, and I would have epically failed my mission because of a mystery boy I met in a museum halfway around the world.

If I went after Damian, I could apprehend him and talk to Hazel Eyes afterwards, having all of my thoughts cleared then.

Yet, Hazel Eyes could disappear while I was gone, and I could miss possibly my only opportunity to get some answers out of this sweet, charming, insanely good looking mystery boy.

I had to make a decision, and I had to make it fast.

I looked Hazel Eyes right in those hazel eyes of his, and I forced the storm of thoughts in my head to calm down enough for me to say, "I'm sorry."

Hazel Eyes gave me a confused look, and as I stepped away from him, he grabbed me by the wrist.

Not forcibly, but gently, he held my wrist and looked at me deeply.

Just moments before had looked at me laid back and charming, now he was serious and urgent.

"Delilah, I *need* to talk to you. I've been needing to talk to you since the hotel lobby. It's really important. Delilah, *please.*" His voice was pressing, emphasizing the significance of what he needed to say to me.

I glanced over at Damian, who looked just about ready to walk away.

I pulled my wrist out of Hazel Eyes' grasp just enough to slip my hand down to his, and I marveled for a moment at how perfectly my hand fit into his, almost as if it were destined to be held in his own.

I looked up at him, and felt a pang of guilt as I looked into his eyes.

I had my mission.

"I'm sorry. It'll have to wait. I'll be back, I promise." I told him, meaning every word.

Hazel Eyes held my hand there for a moment, not letting me leave, but eventually he let me step away, and after a longing glance, I turned around and walked away from my mystery boy.

Damian was already walking away from the waiter and back into the crowd, so I trailed behind at a discreet distance, saying into my comms unit, "I've got eyes on the target. He's heading north towards the front of the room. I'm going to initiate contact and have him brought to the main agents. Can I get backup?"

James answered, "I see you. And I see the subject ahead of you. I'll go help you with the misleading trap. Everyone else, meet up with the main agents to help with the apprehending phase."

My parents and Roy agreed, and James' parents, who were also on the comms line, got into position.

I watched as James emerged from the crowd and fell into step beside me.

Together, we walked up to Damian, and James bumped into him, slipping his hand into Damian's blazer pocket and pulling out his cell phone.

Once James pulled back, he discreetly slipped the phone to me, and I hid it in his blazer pocket.

"I'm so sorry, sir, forgive me. I'm a bit clumsy today." James said, faking an apology.

"No problem, son, it happens," Damian replied, "Just keep an eye out from now on."

James smiled, saying, "Oh, I will, Mr..."

"Donovan. George Donovan." Damian extended a hand towards James, who took it and shook it, and I couldn't help but smile at Damian's alias.

He had no idea he was about to be busted.

Damian gave me a small head bow, acknowledging me.

"Nice to meet you, Mr. Donovan. Say, that's a very nice watch you're wearing." I said, getting right to the point.

Hopefully, he would take the bait.

"Oh, why thank you. It's one in a million, not many other pieces are out there." He replied.

"Oh, really? I know a colleague of mine who would be very interested in a piece like that. He's been searching and searching, looking for information. Would you like us to take you to him? If you don't mind helping us, that is." James asked, perfectly playing the part.

"Helping fellow man and making a potential friend? How could I pass up on such an opportunity? Lead the way." Damian said.

Hook, line, and sinker.

James and I smiled at each other, and we led Damian back to James' parents.

From there, we explained how "Mr. Donovan" knew where to find watches like his own, and James' parents were able to get Damian out of the building with some serious spy influence tactics, and my family was able to surprise him outside with an arrest.

Once I got the all clear from Roy that Damian was arrested and safely apprehended, I started making my way back to Hazel Eyes.

My mission was complete, after all.

James stopped me before I could leave, saying, "Thank you Kay, again, so much. I... really enjoyed seeing you here."

I was touched at his sincerity, and I replied, "You're welcome James. You know I'm always here for you."

And with that, I set out to find Hazel Eyes.

He was still standing by the candelabra, and the look on his face was one of concern as he searched the crowd.

I walked up to him, and Hazel Eyes looked relieved.

"Can I expect any more mad dashes away from me this evening?" He asked, being the definition of charm.

I smiled and said, "No. I'm free to talk, now."

Hazel Eyes walked towards me and took my hand in his, saying, "Good. There's something I need to say to you. But first... May I have this dance?"

I was hesitant, up until this point I had only talked to Hazel Eyes, and now I was going to be dancing with him?

But my strive for answers overruled everything else, so I did something that changed my evening entirely.

I smiled, and said, "You may."

And with that, Hazel Eyes led me to the edge of the crowd of dancers.

He slipped his left hand onto my waist, holding my right hand in his.

My breath caught as I laid my right hand on his shoulder, and looked up at him.

The moment was perfect, both of us searching each other's eyes, searching for answers.

We started to dance, and he began speaking, saying, "I've been thinking a lot about what's been happening lately. With you and I running into each other so frequently. And I..." He trailed off, pressing his lips together slightly and turned his head away from me.

I looked up at him confused, and asked, "What is it?"

Hazel Eyes shook his head, as if clearing his thoughts, and began again, saying, "Nothing. It's just… I never thought I'd be having this conversation."

"The unexpected is what makes life interesting, isn't it? And besides, there's a first time for everything." I pointed out.

Hazel Eyes smiled, and said, "You're right," as he spun me slowly and gently.

He dipped me, and asked, "Can we go outside? This is something I want to say in a more… private manner."

I should have said no.

All of the training I had up to this moment told me *not* to go in a secluded area away from the crowd of people with someone I barely knew.

But with Hazel Eyes, things felt… *different.*

I could sense something in him that wasn't like most other people, and as the world was upside down when he dipped me, so was my judgement.

"Lead the way." I said.

Hazel Eyes set me back on my own two feet and said, "You're surprisingly trusting with me. Why?"

I shrugged and answered, "There's just something about you."

Hazel Eyes stayed looking at me for a long moment, then turned and led the way outside.

Little did I know this conversation would literally change my future.

Chapter Sixteen

*L*uckily, Hazel Eyes took me out to the other side of the building, completely opposite of my parents and Roy.

He led me a little ways off, still near the building, but under the safe cover of some trees, where we were shrouded in shade.

The moon had already made its appearance, and the moonlight cut through the branches and cast odd yet mesmerizing shadows over Hazel Eyes' face.

Once I was with him, he opened his mouth to speak, but couldn't.

He exhaled sharply and put his hand on his neck, taking a few steps back and shaking his head.

"I didn't think this would be so hard." He said, a look of disbelief on his face.

"What is it? Come on, talk to me," I said, desperate for answers.

Hazel Eyes walked around a bit, clearing his thoughts.

I was tempted to start pacing as well, but I stopped myself

before I could.

Tripping and falling in my high heels in front of Hazel Eyes was not on my initial agenda for the evening.

Then again, neither was being with Hazel Eyes.

He sighed then rubbed the side of his jaw, closed his eyes for a moment, and then spoke, saying, "Back in Monaco, at the hotel… Were you looking for someone?"

I wasn't sure how to respond, so I countered, "How odd that were both at the *same* hotel, in the *same* city, in the *same* country, at the *same* time. You said you were looking for someone. Who was it?"

Hazel Eyes looked at me, then said, "You didn't answer my question."

"You didn't answer mine." I countered.

Hazel Eyes pressed his lips together slightly, on the left side of his mouth, then continued, "Ch-. Jared. Jared Donfrey. Ever heard of him? I know you have, Delilah. Please don't deny it. I want the truth."

Hazel Eyes looked at me deeply, so deep I had a hard time thinking straight.

"I think I deserve the truth, too. Who were you looking for?" I asked again.

He sighed, a long, fatigue-filled sigh, before saying, "My brother. I was looking for my brother. Our relationship is… complicated. But it's a relationship nonetheless. I was looking for him."

Hazel Eyes' whole stance seemed to lighten, as if a weight on his shoulders had been lifted.

I tried to process what he had just said.

He was looking for his brother at the hotel.

So what was he doing at the café?

Or the Senatru?

I was about to ask these questions, when he continued, "I told you my part. Now, you. Were you looking for someone? Don't lie, Delilah."

I took a deep breath, unsure how to respond.

Was I really going to tell a stranger what I was doing on my *secret* mission?

I looked at Hazel Eyes, and wondered how he knew about Jared.

I said, "How do you know about Jared Donfrey? *What* do you know?"

Hazel Eyes shook his head at me, saying, "That doesn't matter. I just want to know... Were you looking for him?"

I looked at him for a long time, debating what I was going I say.

If I told him the truth, I would be breaking cover, letting my secret life known to a stranger.

I didn't really have the option of lying; he had already called me out.

I took a deep breath and said, reluctantly, "Yes, I was looking for him."

Hazel Eyes covered his hands with his face, rubbed his eyes, and shook his head, staying deep in thought for a moment.

Finally, he stepped forward, getting closer to me.

"You're with the C.I.A aren't you? Or F.B.I? Wait, what am I saying? You're probably O.U.O." He said, as easily as if we were talking about the weather.

I stayed stunned.

My mind couldn't process what he had just asked.

C.I.A.? F.B.I? *O.U.O?!*

How in the world did he know about *O.U.O?!*

Only a select group of people knew about O.U.O's existence, and most were the people who *worked* for O.U.O!

We all knew each other; there were no strangers in our organization.

How did Hazel Eyes know about us?

"I already answered one of your questions. Now, you answer one of mine. What were you doing at the Senatru museum? I know that the bird statue was stolen. Don't lie to me." I said assertively.

As the words left my mouth, it dawned on me where Hazel

Eyes might have sat in the gala rankings.

There were the genuinely rich, the spies, and…

Well, I didn't want to think about the third option.

Hazel Eyes sighed, then looked at me, carefully choosing his words.

I could tell he was thinking about the right words to get around my question, but when he gave up, he said, "I was there to take the statue."

I felt faint.

I had weighed the possibility, of course, but actually hearing the words come out of his mouth was different from hearing it in my head.

Every fiber in my being was telling me to turn him in.

My spy DNA was telling me to grab his arms, twist him around, knee him in a pressure point on his back, and once he was on the ground, I would tell him his Miranda Rights.
Every molecule I possessed told me to do it.

But my heart didn't.

Deep down I knew he was different, *felt* that he was different.

I just couldn't do it.

Hazel Eyes leaned against a tree and crossed his arms.

He said, "I guess this is the part where you turn me in? Or, arrest me? I'll have you know I can run a mile in 5 minutes flat, so catching me might be hard. But then again, your O.U.O training might give you an advantage…"

"Just, *stop!*" I exclaimed, exasperated.

Hazel Eyes didn't flinch or falter at my outburst, he stayed coolly leaning against the tree, watching me.

"I don't even know your *name*, and all of a sudden I'm meeting you at three different places, I keep getting distracted because of you, you're questioning my affiliations, and you just admitted to me that you *stole* something?! *Who are you?*" I asked, desperate for answers.

Hazel Eyes sighed and rubbed the back of his neck.

He looked at me in his deep way that I was growing accustomed to, and replied, "Jay. My name is Jay. I don't know why I keep running into you, but I know it's probably because our… *tasks*, keep conflicting with each other. I'm not going to lie, I've been having a hard time focusing lately with you on my mind, too. The only thing that makes sense right now is that you work for O.U.O, that's why you've been where you've been. And yes, I took the statue. My motives are a part of who I am."

I shook my head, trying to gather my thoughts.

I was silent for a moment sorting things out in my mind.

His name was Jay.

The way he said it, I knew he was telling the truth.

Jay was a thief.

He knew about O.U.O.

Someway, somehow, our missions were connected.

His motives for stealing has something to do with his persona.

I had been on his mind lately.

"Well… Jay, I'm not sure what to do here. You're outpouring your whole life story to me, and… I'm not sure what to do here." I admitted.

Jay cocked his head and said, "You were trusting with me, so now I'm trusting with you. But now, you might want to start with telling me *your* name."

I looked at him before saying, "Kay. My name is Kay."

Jay smiled for what felt like forever, and he said fondly, "Jay and Kay. What are the odds?"

I laughed a bit at his point, how odd was it that our names were just letter away from being identical.

Jay grew serious, and in a few steps closed the distance between us.

He grabbed my hands and held them in his, before looking at me in his deep way and saying, "I want you to be careful, Kay. I know you've probably been at this for a while, but this business…"

He trailed off, unsure of what to say next.

He continued, saying, "This business is cruel. Everything happens for a reason, everyone meets someone for a reason, and the last thing I want is to see you get hurt. I know some things, Delilah. Things you couldn't fathom. Meeting you, talking to

you, having that mystery person to run into, it's been fun, but...
Please be careful."

He leaned in closer to me, emphasizing 6 words I would never
forget for the rest of my life, "The world is a dangerous place."

He pulled away from me, taking a few steps back, but still
held my hands in his own.

I let his words sink in, realizing that he was trying to protect
me from something, from someone.

Some of the pieces still didn't add up.

"But, Jared Donfrey? What does he have to do with-?"

Jay cut me off, saying, "I've told you, Delilah, be *careful.* Don't
be worrying about things that aren't your priority. I know what
I'm telling you. I've made the connections, and *trust me,* stay
away from things that are out of your hands. I don't want to see
you get hurt."

His warnings were genuine, and I could tell he was telling me
the truth when he said he knew things I didn't.

The part that stumped me was why he chose to come tonight,
and why he was giving me such cryptic warnings about not wanting to see me get hurt.

I looked into those hazel eyes of his and asked, "What are you
doing, here, Jay?"

He pulled me closer and said, in a low voice, "Regretting that
I didn't dance with you sooner, Kay."

In that moment, having my hands in his, his eyes focused on

me, the moonlight cutting shadows onto both of our faces, I felt a surge of an emotion that I can't quite name.

I was caught up in the moment, loving the rush of the craziness of the situation.

Here I was, all dressed up, in the cover of trees with the moon witnessing my hands being cradled in the hands of a boy whose name I had just learned minutes earlier.

He was telling me how he didn't want me hurt, even though he didn't even know who I was.

He held me close to him, closer than I had ever thought we'd be.

I found myself feeling an emotion I tried to suppress; it was too crazy to be feeling that way with a stranger.

Jay looked at me for a long moment, and said, in a low voice, "Please, be careful. I know I don't know anything about you, but still… *be careful*. I'm not like you, I probably never will be. But just know that, to me, you're… different. From the moment I saw you, you were different. Trust me when I say, I don't want to see you hurt."

I looked up at him, watched as the moonlight seemed to make his hazel eyes glow.

I opened my mouth to speak, when Jay's expression changed.

He seemed the slightest bit startled, but he recovered almost instantaneously.

He remained silent, and after a moment gave me an apologetic look.

I glanced at his right ear, and realized that I could just make out a comms unit, peeking out at me.

If you weren't looking for it, you wouldn't have seen it.

But I did.

I looked back at him and asked, "Let me guess, you need to go? You might as well just tell the person on the other line that you're on your way."

Jay seemed surprised that I noticed his quick episode of being caught off guard, and he smiled, saying, "You're good, Delilah. For a moment, I forgot my comms was even there. Just for a moment, though."

He pulled away and let my hands slowly slip away from his, and before he turned to walk away, he looked me in the eyes and said, "Remember. The world is a dangerous place."

And with that, Jay disappeared into the night, under the cover of the trees and shrouded in the shadows.

I stayed there for a moment, trying to fully process what had just happened.

My heart was pounding, and it was taking some time to calm down.

Eventually, I turned and headed back to the gala, trying to figure out how Jay knew Jared, and what "things" he knew about that "I couldn't fathom".

Most of all, I tried to figure out what Jay was trying to protect me from, and why he didn't want to see me hurt.

That was the hardest to wrap my head around.

Once I made it back to the gala, the scene hadn't changed.

Rich people dancing, spies eating, thieves lurking.

I wondered if Jay was still in the crowd somewhere, but I dismissed the thought from my mind.

He was probably long gone by now.

I met up with Roy, and we both congratulated each other on a job well done, and a mission well accomplished.

After our congrats, Roy took a good, long look at me.

"What?" I asked, hoping for once he wouldn't tap into our sibling telepathy.

"I'm getting the vibe that something happened. Something's up with you. What happened?" He asked, assuming the big brother part of his personality.

"I don't really know how to start. I'll just... Tell you at the hotel." I said, meaning my every word.

I was still trying to process what had just happened, I seriously doubted I could explain it all to Roy and *not* sound the slightest bit crazy.

Roy gave me an, 'Ok But You Better Tell Me' look, before dropping the subject and asking to dance with me.

The rest of the night went smoothly; I fluctuated between dancing with Roy and my dad, and I danced with James once.

My mom and I chatted for a bit throughout the night, but besides these distractions, my mind was never far from thinking about Jay.

My head was filled with swirling questions about him, what he was doing at the gala, and what he meant about wanting me to be careful.

I figured, after lots of heavy thinking, to just stop mulling over it and try to have fun.

After all…

I had all the time in the world to wonder about Jay and his cryptic messages.

I had completed my mission; now was the time for happiness and satisfaction, not confusion and headaches.

If the universe wanted Jay and I to meet again, it would happen.

And when it did, our encounter would go smoother and with more answered questions.

I doubted anything would go wrong.

Right?

Chapter Seventeen

The night came to a close and the gala ended, leaving my inevitable conversation with Roy to be dealt with.

As I walked back into the hotel, I could sense his questions, and I knew he was mulling over scenarios of my story in his head.

My family and I changed out of our fancy yet torturous clothing and shoes, and Roy pulled me away down to the pool.

Neither of us got in, we simply slipped off our shoes and let our feet dangle into the water, the water line ending at our ankles.

"So? Tell your big brother the story." Roy urged, prompting me to begin.

I sighed, and rubbed my face in my hands.

I had been debating on how I should start this conversation; after all, I wanted to tell Roy.

I really did.

I just didn't know how he would take it.

"Umm... Ok. Remember that boy from the Senatru

Museum?" I asked.

Roy nodded a slow, big brother-like nod, and the look on his face told me I should continue, but be careful of what I said.

I took a deep breath and said, "Well, after the Senatru, we ran into him at that café in Monaco. And after that…"

"You ran into him at the hotel we searched." Roy finished for me.

My jaw snapped shut as I gave my brother a confused look.

He shrugged, saying, "What? You may be a spy, but I'll always have more experience. "

I waved my hand at him, my signal for telling him to hush.

"Anyway, I *did* run into him, but we didn't say much. All I could get out of him was that he had been looking for someone. After that, I left with you and Mr. G. But the look on his face when we left… I don't know." I said, starting to confuse myself.
"I saw his face. He seemed…" Roy trailed off.

"Disconcerted." Roy and I said in unison.

"Yeah. But… I saw him one other time. Tonight, at the gala." I told him.

Roy leaned forward, as if in anticipation of what I was going to say next.

I started the story, from how Jay found me, how I had to leave to catch Damian, how I came back and we danced, how he led me outside, our conversation, and his departure.

Roy stayed silent for most of my storytelling, his facial expressions rarely changing as I spoke.

Finally, when I finished, he leaned back and rubbed his eyes, processing everything he had just been told.

Roy looked at me, and asked, "And you never went to find me?"

I bit my lip, being both annoyed and nervous that the big brother part of Roy had decided to take the lead on this conversation, not the best friend part.

I never knew which side I was going to get.

I gathered up the courage to say, "I knew you were busy with Damian, and I knew you would get upset like this. I made the call on my own, and-"

"You made the *wrong* call. Kay, he admitted to you that he *stole* something! Are you, or are you not aware, that it is your *job* to turn people like him in. He's a thief. Do you hear me? A *thief.* I can't believe you just let him off the hook like that. I really can't." Roy cut me off.

I bit my lip even harder, and managed to say, "You don't understand. There's something about him that's just... *different.*"

"Yeah, different because he's a *thief.*" Roy interjected.

I glared at him and continued, "I've felt it all along. I think I did the right thing by letting him go. I have a feeling that someway, somehow, we might need him."

Roy scoffed at my idea, saying, "Need him for what? I know I would never trust a thief for anything."

He must have seen the look on my face, because he sighed, and said, "Runt, I thought you were better than this. At O.U.O, I'm always happy to tell people you're my sister. I like knowing that on a mission, you'll have my back and make the best judgement calls, no questions asked. I trust you."

"So, what, you don't trust me anymore? Just because I listened to my gut, which is exactly what you always tell me to do?" I countered.

"I never said I didn't trust you." He replied, in his big brother way.

"Well, it sure feels like you did." I snapped, before biting my lip even more.

"Ugh, you just don't get it. I know that there's something more to him. I can feel it. If you think I'm just an immature kid who doesn't know what she's doing, then fine by me. I know I'm right. There's nothing you can say to change the way I feel." I stood up to leave as I talked, looking down at Roy in one of my few chances to be taller than him.

Bigger than him.

More important than him.

I started to walk away, when suddenly the thought of Roy turning Jay in hit me.

Fear rose up in my throat, when my older brother spoke.

"If that's your call, then fine. I won't say anything. Just know I don't agree. In fact, I'm disappointed." Roy said to my back, tapping into our sibling telepathy.

I didn't turn around.

I simply stopped walking, and let his words sink in.

Roy was going to keep his word.

He always does.

Whatever emotion he felt towards my action, I shouldn't have cared.

So what if he was 'disappointed'?

I shouldn't care what he thought of my judgement calls.

But I did.

I cared very much.

Being back at school was like a breath of fresh air.

I was glad I had a distraction from my hurt feelings with Roy, and I was especially glad that the oncoming cold weather meant more indoor classes away from the chilly winds, and lots and lots of hot chocolate from the cafeteria.

By this time of the year, November, northern winds were blowing in and my little town was starting to shiver.

The thing I loved about Texas was how hot it gets.

For me, 70 degrees is sweater weather.

80 degrees, we're getting there.

90 degrees, perfect.

However, in the spanning months of November through January, the weather took a turn for the cold, and I had to admit, I hated it.

If I had my way, winter would be 70 degrees the entire time, cool, but not cold.

I would trade all of my cups of hot chocolate for the day in exchange for an hour of 90 degree heat during the winter.

Scarlet thought otherwise.

"I already know what the answer is going to be, but do you want to sit outside today?" She asked cheerfully.

I glared at her incredulously, and replied, "Um, how about no?"

Scarlet nodded, "Fair enough. No one will be out there anyway. I don't understand how so many people can hate the cold. It's a *gift*! Time away from the tortuous, scorching sun and its scalding heatwaves!"

I laughed at Scarlet's little monologue, and replied, "The cold most definitely is *not* a gift. It's a tortuous, shivering wave of bitter sadness filled with the sniffles, coughs, and heavy, itchy sweaters that are hidden away in your closet all year except for right now. It doesn't even snow here! How could you crave such horrific weather that doesn't even do anything special?"

Scarlet shook her head at me, "My poor, dear best friend. How I wish you could see the beauty before you."

I shivered before replying, "My delusional, dear best friend. How I wish you could stop pointlessly arguing and eat your meal."

Scarlet frowned and bit into her chicken sandwich.

We were sitting inside, eating at a small, round table on the right side of the cafeteria.

I knew James was going to come and sit with us, as he always did when we sat inside.

That talk might have been in German or Swahili, but who really cared if we all understood each other?

Sure enough, James found his way over to our table and sat down to my left and Scarlet's right.

Scarlet and I were sitting across from each other, and James was on the side.

"Hey." I said, nodding as he sat down.

"Hi." He replied, digging into his spaghetti.

Scarlet stayed chewing her sandwich, and she and James exchanged small smiles.

I took a look around, watching my fellow peers as they bustled about the cafeteria.

I'm sure the spy side of Henderson had something to do with it; every little group and clique of people consisted of two to four people. Never one, never more than four.

The larger groups of four usually consisted of people who

shared a common interest. Like, with all of their hearts.

Smaller groups of two and three were just very good friends who enjoyed each other's company.

There was never anyone sitting alone at Henderson.

We were always together, but not in big groups.

The students at Henderson may have been cut into their small sections, but we were all one big, happy, spy family.

"So, are you excited for PE today? The Soccer Unit is almost over, and I know that we're doing basketball next." James said, in between bites of his spaghetti.

"We have to walk from here to the gym, *outside*. That part, I'm not looking forward to." I replied.

Scarlet playfully shook her head at me, then asked, "So, what are your plans for Thanksgiving break, James?"

James swallowed his bite of spaghetti before answering, "We're just going to stay here for Thanksgiving. My aunts and uncles are visiting us this year, so the meal is going to be at our house."

Scarlet and I nodded at his response.

James jutted his chin out towards us, and asked, "What about you two?"

Scarlet replied, "I'm pretty much doing the same thing as you. Staying here, spending time with the family. My grandparents live one town away, so we're going to visit them there."

James turned to me, asking, "What about you, Kay?"

I held off taking a bite of my pizza to respond, "Unless something *unexpected,* comes up, I should spend my vacation here. We'll have our meal, then sleep… Eat leftovers, then sleep… The cycle repeats until school starts again."

James laughed, and smiled at my response.

The rest of the day went on normally.

PE came and went, with satisfying victory after a soccer match followed by high fives from my teammates.

AP Chemistry was filled with fun and fear as Mr. Needlemeyer demonstrated how to create a miniature explosive using tin foil, chocolate, batteries, and matches.

Upon my arrival at home, I found Roy asleep on the sofa, his laptop open in front of him.

I pressed the space bar to wake up the screen, and Roy's email greeted me.

I didn't mean to snoop, but what can I say? Spying is in my blood.

I scanned the page, and my heart sunk when I realized Lenox hadn't given my brother any word yet.

Roy stirred, and woke up shortly after that, greeting me and setting off to the kitchen to grab a bag of chips.

After our heated talk after the gala, things were a little tense between us.

Things went back to normal quickly, as they always did with us, and we were back to our normal sibling routine.

He threw a pillow at me while I was working out a particularly tricky calculus problem, and I stole his chip bag and tossed it onto a shelf across the room.

The rest of my week was uneventful, the normal routine coming and going.

What happened the week after that, during Thanksgiving break, was anything but normal.

Chapter Eighteen

*Y*ou might think that being given the assignment to go and sneak into a secret meeting filled with criminals with your brother and best friend would be exciting...

But I was scared.

After my last run in with Jay, I was nervous over what I might come to face.

His warnings for me to be careful echoed in my head as Roy informed me of our mission, we packed up, said goodbye to parents, hopped on a plane, and landed in Detroit, Michigan.

The entire way, from learning what we had to do to walking up to the crime oozing building, Jay's words swirled in my head.

He cared about me, even though he didn't really even know me.

Why was he so centered on me being careful, and me getting involved in things I shouldn't?

Why did he care so much?

Why did I care so much?

I shook my thoughts away, trying to get myself to focus on my mission, and stop thinking about Jay.

I didn't know why Jay had such a grip on my mind.

Usually, nothing could stop me from being 100% absorbed in my mission.

But with Jay, I couldn't help myself.

He never seemed to be far from my mind.

Roy could sense I had something on my mind; he would glance my way, and give me looks of question.

I would give him looks of reassurance in response, telling him not to worry.

But I knew he was still suspicious.

Roy, Scarlet, and I all walked up to an abandoned factory, staying shrouded in the shadows.
It was 10:30 at night, and we had been watching the factory since 5.

O.U.O had received intel that some of the worst crime bosses in the north would be converging at this factory tonight, to discuss an upcoming plan that would start soon.

Our mission was to sneak in, undetected, and see what we could learn about the upcoming crime.

"Okay. I'll go in through the left, Runt, you take right, and Scarlet, you go in through here. We'll sneak around and see what we can find, then all listen in on the meeting. The comms link is on manual mode, and only, and I mean *only* use it in an emergency. We can't afford making a single sound and risking getting caught. Am I clear?" Roy asked, his voice booming with authority and strength.

Scarlet nodded, and I replied, "As crystal."

Roy gave a single nod at us, and looked back at the building.

I knew that his internal clock was synced with my own, and we had planned to break in at 10:35, a short while before the crime meeting would take place.

We all stayed there quietly, watching and listening for anything suspicious.

As time went by, I had less and less trouble keeping Jay off my mind.

I would simply remind myself that some of the worst crime bosses in America would be under the same roof as I was tonight, and if I made one wrong move, I would be like a canary in a cage full of cats.

That was a good incentive to stay on task.

When my internal clock hit 10:34, Roy and I nodded to each other, and we set out for our sides of the building, while Scarlet stayed put.

I headed to the right of the building, making sure to stay covered in the shadows, and avoided any security cameras that caught my eye.

By the time I got to the right of the building, I knew it was 10:35, and I started opening a low window so I could slip inside.

My black gloves made opening the window the slightest bit more difficult than it should have been, but I managed to make it in.

I slid inside of the building, and was grateful for a long row of wooden crates to hide behind.

I silently stepped onto the floor and dropped to my hands and knees.

I began crawling to the nearest staircase, taking quick glances through the cracks in the boxes to see my surroundings.

The room was empty, and the only light in the building came in from the street lamps and lights outside through the windows.

I managed to make it to the staircase as silently as I could have hoped, and I tested the sounds of the staircase by placing a single foot on the bottom stair and applying pressure.

The staircase was made of old, rusted metal, and the slightest bit of my weight didn't make a sound.

I became hopeful, but when I pressed harder, the stairs creaked and moaned in a completely screeching and undesirable way.

I winced and ducked back down to my hiding place, hoping that no one would walk in to see where the noise came from.

Lucky for me, it was a large, old factory that the crime bosses decided to meet in, so I doubt they heard the stairs.

I had to find the room where the meeting was taking place, so I pulled myself up and over one of the wooden crates to make it to the main ground floor.

A door greeted me on the other side of the room, so I stayed close to the walls as I stealthily made my way over to it.

Once I was out of the room, I explored other areas of the right side of the factory, trying to find the meeting and anything else that could help me on my mission.

A search of a room filled with conveyor belts revealed that the factory must have been shut down and abandoned abruptly, since there were still crates sitting atop the machinery.

After I walked around another section for a bit, checking inside of crates and boxes, I learned that the factory used to assemble and package calculators.

I grabbed one out of one of the old, weathered, beat up boxes, and slipped it deep into my front pocket.

It was small enough to fit inside perfectly, and I knew there was no chance of it slipping out.

Why waste a perfectly good souvenir?

I silently rummaged around the factory some more, trying to find where the crime bosses were at.

Our source had stated that the meeting wouldn't start until 11:00, and at that time it was 10:47.

I had about 13 minutes left before the main event, so I had to keep looking.

I stumbled upon a small room that seemed to be an office of sorts.

An old, silver filing cabinet stood tall in the corner, and when

I pulled on the drawer handles, they held shut.

They were locked up tight.

I slipped a lock pick out from a pouch on my utility belt, and in less than 22 seconds, I had all six drawers unlocked.

I pilfered through the drawers, coming to the conclusion that the only paperwork inside dealt with packaging costs and revenue being gained from the factory's operation.

Nothing that could hint at what the crime bosses were planning.

I went through the desk, trying to find anything especially interesting.

I came up empty handed; all I could find was more documents restating what I had just read earlier.

I silently sighed, rearranged the room to the way it was before I found it, and continuing on my way to find the crime bosses meeting.

I stumbled upon a large area, filled with crates and boxes from floor to ceiling.

The room was missing its door, an empty slot sat lonely as the room lay inside.

I took in the entire room, trying to see if I could find a way to the next room.

The boxes definitely made it tricky, but luckily, I enjoyed a good challenge.

I walked about 5 feet away from the door, and three feet into the room.

A strange feeling settled in my stomach, but I couldn't quite place what it was.

All I knew was that my gut was trying to tell me something.

I semi-waved the feeling away, trying to focus on finding the meeting.

I kept my senses on high alert though, just in case anything were to happen.

I placed my foot on top of a box, testing its strength, and when I determined it could hold my weight, I started pushing myself up to climb onto a crate.

But I never made it.

The next thing I knew, two hands were on my waist, pulling me back down on solid ground.

Instinct took over, and I swung my right leg out, and then back in, striking my attacker hard on the back.

I used that momentum to whirl around as much as I could, grabbing the hands that were holding me in the process.

I was about to kick again and pry the hands off of my waist, when I saw the face of the person holding me.

I stopped instantly, stunned, and in disbelief.

My attacker (if you could really call them that) lifted one hand from my waist and rose it to their own mouth, holding a finger to their lips to signal quiet.

I released my grip on their remaining hand, and stood on my two feet.

I waited for them to let go of my waist, but they kept their hand there, resting, as if securing me to that spot.

I stayed looking at them, unsure whether to hug them, or punch them.

"I've always had respect for girls who can take care of themselves," they whispered.

Jay rubbed his back where I had kicked him, and he winced when he rubbed a particularly tender spot.

I didn't know what to say.

I had finally managed to get Jay out of my head, and here he was, standing right in front of me.

With his hand on my waist.

Rubbing the spot where I had just kicked him in an attempt to escape his grasp.

Are you kidding me?

He must have seen the look of guilt on my face, because he gave me a small smile and whispered, "Relax, Delilah. I've been through worse. I'll survive."

I gave a small huff to show my disbelief, and I asked, "What are you doing here?"

Jay shrugged, and replied, "Same as you. Although I wish I could say I wasn't. Didn't I warn you to stay away from things that don't involve you?"

My eyes must have flared at that moment, because the look on Jay's face changed.

His expression changed from concern to... well... fear.

"Are you kidding?" I hissed, my voice still a whisper, "Are you *kidding*? Did you honestly think I would stop *doing my job* just because you told me to? I could have really hurt you if I hadn't recognized you. And what do you mean by 'same as you'?!"

Jay stopped rubbing his back for a moment to exhale deeply, and looked at with his deep gaze.

"I'm sorry. I know that what you do out here is none of my business. I just... Don't want to see you get hurt, or worse. I've been on this side of the field for a while; I know things you don't. And you're right. I was dumb to think you'd stop or even hesitate just because I said something. I'm sorry I startled you," he paused to rub his back again, "that probably was a bad call on my part." Jay's apology was genuine. I could see it in his eyes.

I felt like the biggest jerk on the planet for snapping at him; he had good intentions.

I sighed before replying, "I'm sorry too. If I had known it was you, I wouldn't have lashed out like that. But my question still stands: what do you mean by, 'same as you'?"

Jay finally let his hand slip away from my waist as he ran his hand through his hair.

He wasn't wearing the leather jacket I had gotten used to

seeing on him, instead, he was wearing a tight dark gray t-shirt, with black jeans and brown boots.

He looked at me, and I imagined him taking in my fitted black t-shirt, black jeggings, and dark gray ankle boots, complete with my gloves.

"You're here for the meeting, aren't you?" Jay asked slowly, pacing his words.

I nodded silently, and my internal clock told me that it was now 10:53.

I had to find that meeting.

Before I could say anything, Jay sighed, long and hard, and rubbed the top bridge of his nose.

"You shouldn't be here, Delilah."

His words stirred something inside of me, although I can't quite name the feeling.

Was I touched? Angry? Confused?

Or something more?

I bit my lip and shook my head, and I sharply retorted, "I know the world is a dangerous place. I'm a big girl. I can take care of myself. Now, this is my *job* we're talking about here. I can't just say no when I'm given an assignment."

Jay sighed once more, and replied, "I know. I know. But that doesn't change my opinion. You don't know what can happen when you mess with the wrong-"

"Shhh." I cut Jay off by shushing him, and placing a finger in the air to quiet him down.

"No, I will not 'shhh'. You need to understand-"

"I'm serious, *shhh!*" I cut him off again, straining to hear the sound that caught my attention.

Jay must have realized that I actually heard something rather than just wanted him to shut his mouth; he walked up closer to me, placing a hand on my shoulder and leaning his head close to mine, as if being at my level would help him hear better.

"What is it?" Jay asked after a moment of silence.

I closed my eyes to concentrate better on finding the source of the muffled noise I had heard.

The noises were at different pitches, sometimes long, sometimes short, and I bit my lip in frustration that I couldn't pin point exactly where it was coming from.

Finally, I found it.

"There." I whispered, pointing to the air shaft overhead to the right.
"There are voices coming through there. Which means…"

"The meeting must be in the next room." Jay finished my sentence for me.

We both took a look at each other, before silently beginning to make our way up to the shaft, climbing over crates and boxes in an attempt to reach the ducts.

I got there first, and was already trying to tug at the metal covering to come free.

It was up higher than I would have liked, and I had to jump to grab a hold of it.

I tugged and pulled before dropping to my feet, then related the process over again.

Years of age and rust made it more difficult than it should have been, but Jay helped me by jumping up with me, and together with one hard pull, the frame came off cleanly, and almost noiselessly.

Jay smiled at our handiwork, and he pulled himself up into the shaft first, his biceps flexing with the effort.

I tried not to swoon and climbed in after him, and together we made our way over to the next room.

The shaft was the slightest bit roomy, and I was glad it was big enough so that my claustrophobic side didn't get the best of me.

Jay crawled ahead of me, turning when needed, and he paused every once in a while. To do what, I don't know; but, he always got back to crawling when it was over.

He finally stopped at a metal vent frame, and motioned for me to come look.

I was careful not to get too close, and I held my arm out to silently signal he shouldn't either.

The last thing I needed was to have the big bad criminals see our shadows from overhead, or worse, the frame give way and we fall smack into their meeting.

I took in all of the faces in the room, mentally registering and memorizing every face I came across.

There were 8 men total, all gathered around an old, metal table that adorned a bottle of whiskey, cups, and cigars.

The electricity was working, but the lights were on only in that room.

No central air traveled through the ducts, and I could have sworn I saw Jay start to sweat the slightest bit.

One of the perks of living in Texas: Heat almost never bothers you.

The men were talking and laughing, and each one had various tattoos on either their arms, face, or both.

I recognized two of them as drug dealers, three as arms smugglers, and two as heads of burglar rings.

The last one I didn't recognize.

Jay crawled the slightest bit forward to get a closer look, being careful not to cast a shadow.

In the confined space, we were closer than anticipated, and I could smell his cologne; subtle, yet there, and it smelled very, *very* good.

I knew that by that time it was 11:00 on the dot, and as if on cue, the one crime boss I didn't recognize rose to his feet.

"Thank you all for meeting here to discuss our future operations. I've been waiting for this meeting for a long time. Technically speaking, we should already start discussing our plans, but it appears we are still missing a colleague. We can wait... For a moment." The man was tall, strongly built, and tan, with a barbed wire tattoo circling his left wrist.

I glanced at Jay, who looked at the man with a look so harsh and full of ill intent, I physically flinched.

He noticed my movement, and he turned to look at me.

His hazel eyes softened, and he whispered in a low tone, "What's wrong?"

I shook my head, still rattled at seeing him with so much hate in his eyes.

I hoped I never saw him with that look again.

"Nothing, it's just... Do you know who he is?" I whispered back as low as I could.

Jay glanced down towards the man, and his eyes flashed with anger.

He nodded slightly before looking back at me, the negativity in his gaze gone once I came into view.
"He's not a good man." He answered, his voice so low I almost didn't hear him.

"Who is he?" I asked, hoping I could get some answers.

Jay shook his head, not looking at me, or at the meeting below us.

"He's not a good man." Jay repeated.

I bit my lip, and looked back down at the meeting.

Jay caught on to my irritation, and he whispered, "Sorry. He's... not a good man. He deals with any and every crime imaginable, from heists to smuggling. He's done some very bad things in his lifetime, and I have no doubt in my mind that he'll continue to do worse. To him, money is the magic word. He would trade his own flesh and blood for a pretty penny. His greed..."

Jay shook his head, as if he wasn't sure what to say.

"His greed is horrific." Jay finished.

I turned to look at the man down below, seeing him a new light.

"Have you ever met him?" I asked.

Jay nodded, "Once. His language is vulgar. He treats you like a piece of dirt, even though he may have just met you. He's crazy. You can tell just by looking him in the eyes."

I sat back, trying to process what Jay was telling me and apply it to the man below me.

"Do you know his name?" I asked after a few seconds.

Jay shook his head, "No. No one really does. Everyone calls him..."

Jay stopped mid-sentence, and lifted his head, as if something had just dawned on him.

"What?" I asked, curious over his sudden pause.

Jay shook his head again, "Nothing."

"Tell me." I replied, moving closer to him.

"It's nothing, Delilah. I don't want you involved with that man any more than you already are. He's *not* a good man." Jay whispered, looking down at the people below.

"Jay, I'm on a *mission*. It's my assignment to learn about the people here and what they're planning. Now, what is his name?" I asked, with as much assertion you can have when whispering.

Jay looked at me for a good, long while, his deep gaze only getting deeper.

"You're a fiery one, aren't you?" He asked, a smile playing on his lips.

I nodded strongly, and replied, "I'm not easily ignored. You should know this about me. Now, I'm going to ask again. What, is his name?"

Jay looked at me fondly, before whispering, "Like I said, no one really knows his real name. In the thieving game, he's known as Xander. Short for Alexander the Great, he thinks he's rules the world."

Jay looked down at Xander for a moment, "He doesn't know how wrong he is."

I looked down at Xander as well, slowly sinking into my own thoughts.

"It's not fair." I whispered, so low I thought only I heard myself.

Jay turned in my direction, his eyes fixated on me.

I looked back at him, unsure what to say; I didn't think he would have heard me.

He stayed looking at me, deep in thought, with a far away, yet deep gaze.

Neither of us spoke for a few minutes, we just stayed there, lost in each other's gazes.

Finally, after what felt like an eternity of swimming in his hazel eyes, Jay whispered, "I know."

He looked at me for a while longer, and I was about to speak, when Xander's booming voice interrupted from below.

"Ahh, Mazder, my good man. Nice of you to show up. *Finally.*" Xander's voice dripped with sarcasm, and even from above I could see the wild look in his eyes.

"Traffic in Detroit. Not my thing." The man known as Mazder replied. I recognized him to be another arms dealer, and he seemed to be the only one without discernible tattoos. He spoke with a French accent, subtle, yet noticeable.

"Well, you're here now, so let us begin, if that *is* your thing." Xander said meanly.

I leaned forward the slightest bit, ready to listen to their meeting, when I spotted movement from the opposite side of the room.

There, shrouded in the dark, so hidden I thought my eyes were playing tricks on me, was Scarlet.

She picked the perfect hiding spot; unable to be seen except from above.

She had crawled in through a window a few feet away, and had nestled into the corner to observe the meeting.

I smiled absently, and when Jay saw my expression, he whispered, "You know her?" He jutted his chin out towards Scarlet down below.

I nodded, still smiling.

"I know her very, very well." I replied.

No sooner had I finished my sentence, my attention was drawn towards the balcony on the left side of the room, almost completely hidden with crates and boxes.

There, crouched Roy, surveying the scene below.

Our sibling telepathy really surprised me sometimes; even when we weren't trying, we still thought on the same wavelength.

Watch from above.

It took a full minute for Jay to notice Roy after I did, and he leaned back in his kneeling position.

He shook his head before whispering, "I should have guessed. You can't have one without the other."

I raised an eyebrow, asking, "What, siblings can't always be together?"

A look of sadness washed over Jay's expression for a fleeting moment, so quick I thought I imagined it.

But I didn't.

Jay shook his head, his face blank, and whispered back, "That's not what I meant."

I didn't know what to say, so I didn't say anything; I simply looked back down at the meeting and listened in to the crime bosses' plans.

Little did I know, those plans would put me in some serious trouble later on.

Chapter Nineteen

"We all know why we're here. To discuss business. Our business is different from the common man's business. No, our business is the business of crime. Some may call us thieves, some crooks, etc., etc. But I know who we really are. People who are just trying to stay at the top of the food chain, that's who we are. Now, what info do you have for me so we can stay the top dogs?" Xander spoke, taking unnecessary dramatic pauses and using hand gestures to exaggerate his mini monologue.

One man in a black jacket and slacks, raised his glass before speaking, "A new little group of arms dealing wanna-bees came in, trying to sell on *my* turf. Let's just say... We took care of them." He gave a sly look to another arms dealer and they both chuckled.

Xander's face grew what can only be described as a scowl that resembled a smile, and he replied mischievously, "Excellent. Anyone else with other good news? Or are you all just failures?"

One drug dealer spoke up, saying, "My income has really spiked since we *spiced up* the product we're selling. We upped the price to, making things even more interesting. Business is booming. You were right to propose the change."

Xander rolled his eyes in disgust, "Uh, tell me something I *don't* know."

The meeting continued on, with Xander asking more questions, and the crime bosses talking about how each of their "businesses" was doing.

One arms dealer reported problems in the north due to a certain gang that was trying to prove themselves to his men, and one heist organizer told the story of how one of their jobs was almost ruined due to lack of communication with a neighboring heist group.

To these, Xander listened intently, and then slammed them with obvious solutions to their problems, so simple you thought they would never have worked.

One arms dealer and one drug dealer managed to slip up and we learned the locations of their base of operations.

Another heist organizer voiced an upcoming job, target, date, and all, set to take place in New York at one of the most heavily guarded banks in the state.

Other small details, like names of collaborators were revealed, and I input all of this data into my HoloWatch, while also keeping it inside my photographic memory.

Jay did the same, only he input all of the information in a small pocket tablet, like a computer, but holographic and much more portable.

It was cutting edge technology, and *really* cool.

Finally, Mazder spoke, after not having said anything in a long time.

"You all… Depress me." Mazder voiced, leaning back in his chair.

Xander turned on him, giving him a piercing look before saying, "Excuse you?"

Mazder shrugged, and repeated, "You heard me. You all depress me."

Xander cocked his head and turned entirely towards Mazder, who seemed to be the only one willing to challenge Xander.

"Oh, my sincerest of apologies. I wasn't aware that our *livelihood* was as sad as a sack of potatoes to you. Tell me, Mazder… Why, *exactly*, do we… *depress* you?" Xander spat the words like venom at Mazder, clearly not fond of being insulted.

Mazder crossed one leg over the other, and leaned forward in his seat, eyeing Xander before saying, "I know men. Large men, with larger crime businesses, larger amounts of workers, larger amounts of jobs, and larger amounts of money than all of you combined. You all are supposed to be the best in the business. But from what I've observed this evening, you are… How do you say? Mediocre."

Xander's right eye twitched twice before he said, in a low voice, "Mediocre?" A pause. "Mediocre." He repeated at normal level. "Mediocre." He said louder, with odd confidence. "Mediocre!" He bellowed and guffawed, as if it were the funniest thing he'd ever heard in his life.

He really looked like a mad man.

In an instant, he stopped laughing and was nose to nose with Mazder, hissing, "And what exactly do those 'large men' you speak of do that's *better* than us? Hm? Why are *they* so *special?*!"

He spat out the last word with so much rage, it sounded like he was wheezing.

Mazder calmly placed a hand on Xander's shoulder, and pushed him away, earning a gasp from one of the drug dealers.

Xander eyed the spot where Mazder's hand lay, as if in disbelief that it was there.

Mazder took his hand away, and folded both hands in his lap.

Mazder spoke with passion, "Those large men are planning something big. Something so huge, so bold, so amazingly brilliant, I cannot speak of it myself, I would not do it justice. Besides, your idle mind couldn't comprehend the genius of it anyhow."
Xander's nostrils flared, and he clenched his fists.

"Say that again. I *dare you*." Xander challenged.

Mazder ignored his anger and continued, "What they have planned will go down in history. It's unheard of, unique, and will wreak havoc and destruction, making it all the more memorable. The payoff will be amazing as well, no doubt. Paris will never be the same."

Jay and I looked at each other, a million questions running through both of our heads.

What was this guy talking about?

What could be so amazing, he couldn't talk about it?

What destruction was he talking about?

Who was behind this?

What could we do about it?

Where in Paris was this happening?

When was this happening?

Why did Jay keep glancing at me when he thought I didn't notice?

Xander stayed looking at Mazder for a long time, and he began to circle him, like a wild animal before pouncing on his prey.

Finally, he stopped mid stride, and said, "Well, tell your big boy friends that I do not take kindly to being insulted by the likes of *you*. You think you're so high and mighty, what, just because you're European? Because you're *French?* You are a *guest* here in this meeting. Or at least, you were. You know, before you insulted our work. Now, I must ask you to leave. The meeting is adjourned, and I must insist that you're the first one out the door. I hope you hit a lamp post on the way back home."

Xander smiled, and finished his drink before taking a seat.

Mazder looked every single person in the eye, before standing and saying, "You all are blind. You can do so much better, but you stay stuck in your old ways. How pitiful."

And with that, Mazder turned and walked out of the room, leaving his full glass of whiskey behind.

I pressed my lips together, unsure of what to think about what Mazder had said.

We stayed in the vent, watching until the last man had left the room.

After a moment of silence, my comms unit crackled in my ear.

"Okay, since the meeting is over, let's keep searching the factory, in case we find anything else. We'll rendezvous back here in 45 minutes." Roy spoke through the comms link.

I reached up to my ear and activated the unit, while I replied, "Sounds good, Chief. I'll keep up with my side."

Jay glanced at me, a single eyebrow raised.

I jutted my chin towards Roy down below, and Jay nodded.

"Alright, I'll keep up with my side then, too." Scarlet agreed.

"Then it's settled. Rendezvous when I said. Chief out." Roy signed off from our conversation and I watched as he disappeared from the balcony, probably out a window.

Scarlet made herself scarce as well, and Jay and I remained inside of the vent together.

"You didn't turn me in." Jay spoke softly, his hazel gaze focused on my own green eyes.

"Well, yeah. You said it yourself, you think I'm different. I feel the exact same way about you. Turning you in felt like…"

"The wrong thing to do?" Jay finished for me.

I nodded, saying, "Exactly."

"I know all about that," Jay gave me a smile so sweet and authentic, I was grateful that I was already sitting because I seriously could have fainted.

Jay turned to crawl back out before saying, "Come on. We can continue searching 'your side' of the factory."

I raised an eyebrow at him, asking, "We?"

Jay shrugged, "I don't see the harm in teaming up."

I sighed before replying, "I suppose I don't either."

I followed him back to the room we had originally entered the shaft from, and Jay climbed out first.

I was lowering myself down onto a crate, when my nerves got the best of me; my grip slipped and I found myself falling.

Jay caught me by the waist, in record time before I could loudly land on the crate below.

He held me there in his grasp, his hazel eyes lost in my green gaze.

"Got you." He said softly, as if speaking too loudly would shatter the moment.

My face was a centimeter away from his, and I was afraid he could hear my heart pounding.

I looked at him, the severity of the craziness of the situation dawning on me.

Here I was, on a mission, searching an abandoned factory with a boy I knew almost nothing about, whom I should have turned in for theft charges; but, instead I was in his arms, about to complete my mission with him as my partner.

My life was insane.

But would I really want it any other way?

After a moment, he let me go, and the space in between us grew until I was no longer in his arms.

"Thanks." I said softly, scared to say the wrong thing and ruin whatever hung in the air between us.

"What are friends for?" He replied smoothly.

I cocked my head and crossed my arms in fake defiance, "Oh, you think we're friends?" I asked playfully.

Jay gave me a sly smile before replying, "Well, we're not enemies, now are we?"

I pretended to think deeply about it, tapping my chin before saying, "No, I suppose not."

Jay grinned before replying, "Then, by process of elimination, that makes us friends. Wouldn't you agree?"

I began climbing down the boxes and crates to the solid ground below before saying, "I think we're great acquaintances, at best."

Jay placed a hand over his heart, and pretended to be wounded, "That hurts, Delilah. You questioning our friendship really hurts, you know that?"

I glanced up at him as he began to climb down after me, and I said, "Oh, how will I ever deal with the guilt?"

Jay speed climbed until he was level with me, and answered, "You can start by making it up to me."

I raised an eyebrow, and asked, "And how exactly would I do that?"

Jay stopped climbing, which prompted me to stop as well.

His expression grew serious as he said, "By helping me find out what's happening in Paris. Maybe even helping me stop it."

I blinked, unsure what to say. Heck, I didn't know what to think.

"What are you doing here, Jay?" I asked, surprising Jay by going off topic.

"I already told you, I'm here for the same reason you are. To learn about what those criminals were planning, and get as much inside information as I could." He answered honestly and unwavering, and my heart fluttered.

"Why?" I asked, sensing that now was the time to get my questions answered; he couldn't just climb away from me, he said it himself: we were working together on this one.

Jay pressed his lips together in that adorable way of his, putting more pressure on the left side of his mouth, before replying, "It's complicated."

I bit my lip before saying sharply, "Everything is complicated with you, isn't it?"

Jay looked at me for a moment, as if processing his thoughts before saying, "Didn't you say that you *liked* complicated?"

I bit my lip even more and replied, "Yes, but not when it's used as an excuse. And certainly not when it comes with lies."

Jay almost lost his grip on the crate he was holding, and my heart skipped a beat at the thought of him falling.

Clearly what I said had taken him aback.
"You think I'm lying to you?" He asked, not even trying to hide the pain in his voice.

I shook my head, and didn't look into his gaze, responding, "I don't know what to think."

Jay shifted as close to me as he could without making both of us lose our grips, and he looked at me deeply before saying, "I may be a thief, but I'm not a liar. Not to you. Do you believe me?"

I searched his face, the spy part of me instructing me to find any tell-tale signs of lying behavior.

But the girl part of me told me he was telling the truth, not needing to check his hand movements, pupils, or mouth pattern.

The girl side of me just needed my heart.

I looked into his eyes and replied, "I do."

Jay gave a single nod, and stayed lost in my gaze before shifting away and continuing the climb back down.

"So, will you help me?" He asked, testing with his foot whether or not a box was safe to step on.

I stayed quiet, not answering until we were back on solid ground.

Jay didn't move once we had reached the floor, instead, he stayed watching me, awaiting my response.

"Why do you care so much about me?" I asked seriously, trying my best to look at him as deeply as he looked me.

"I mean, you don't even *know* me. Yet, you treat me like I've been in your life for years. I didn't even know your *name* until our last run in at the gala. So I'm asking, why do you care?"

I could see his eyes soften, as if my words caused him to temporarily change being, as if he wasn't a thief standing in front of me; no, he was just a boy with a girl asking him a question.

After a moment, he answered, "If I told you, you wouldn't believe me."

I bit my lip, and after a moment, shook my head.

I silently turned and began to walk out of the room.

My internal clock told me I had 37 minutes left before I had to meet with my brother and best friend, so I started walking.

"Delilah, wait." Jay reached out and grabbed my hand in his, and I had an involuntary flashback to the gala.

I turned to him and asked, "What?"

He looked at me intently, his expression nothing but serious.

"All you need to know, is that I care about you. The why isn't important. No matter how much I don't want you hurt, I would still like your help. And you're right, I don't know you. But I would like to. Say you'll help me?" His grip on my hand tightened, and he took a step closer to me.

I don't know why I did what I did next.

Roy would have strangled me if he had been there; another

case of making the wrong judgement call.

I looked at Jay for a long time, processing my thoughts before replying, "Yes. Yes, I'll help you."

Jay let out a breath, one I could tell not even he knew he was holding.

"Great… Great. With you, we're sure to stop whatever is going to happen." Jay let my hand go, and he started walking towards the exit the same way I had.

I walked next to him, a comfortable silence sitting between us as we left the room and began to search other areas within the factory.

We stumbled upon a room filled with old computers and filing cabinets, so we started to pilfer.

My mind raced as the why, how, where, and when aspects of helping Jay swirled in my head.

I had just agreed to help a thief stop other criminals.

Since Jay was doing something good, did that really make him bad?

Why did Jay want to stop other criminals, when he himself wasn't a clean slate?

How was I going to help him, if I had a million other things to do and knew absolutely *nothing* about his life?

Where would I help him, since this incident was taking place in Paris?

When would I talk to him, meet with him, *help* him?

Jay must have had these questions in his head too, because he stopped going through a pile of manila folders and reached into his pocket.

He walked over to me and grabbed my hand, palm upturned.

He placed the item he was holding into it, and said, "Here. It's a satellite communicator. Wherever you may be, just flip it open and press the pad, you can call me through this. It has other features too, but I'll let you figure those out for yourself. Wouldn't want to take all of the fun out of it."

I looked down at the smooth, round object that now lay in my hand.

It was light blue, with darker blue accents and seemed to be brand new.

"It looks like a compact…" I flipped it open as he instructed, and continued, "It *is* a compact. Why would you have this with you?"

Jay shrugged, and replied, "I was hoping I would run into you again."

I blushed before closing it, and extended my hand back to him.

"I can't accept this. We'll find some other way to communicate, I don't want to rob you of something I know is a ridiculously expensive piece of technology." I held it out to him to take back, looked at him earnestly.

Jay shook his head, and gently pushed my hand back

towards me.

"Trust me, we'll need to stay in touch. It's not robbing me if I give it to you. Besides, I'm already asking for a lot by helping me stop a crime occurring halfway around the world. I think we're even." Jay smiled, letting me know it was okay.

I looked back down at the compact in my hands, and asked, "How do I know it's not just a tracking device, or a drone?"

Jay laughed - yes, actually laughed - before smiling at me.

"You're paranoid, you know that? And you know, you ask a lot of questions." Jay nodded towards the compact in my hands, and said, "Trust me, Delilah. I'm not lying to you."

I looked from him to the compact, sorting through my thoughts.

Finally, I slipped the compact into my pocket, looked Jay straight in the eye, and replied, "I know."

Our search continued on until my internal clock told me we had 5 minutes left.
I told Jay how much time we had, and together we made our way out of the factory.

We had both turned out empty handed; neither of us had found anything particularly special, let alone something that could provide information on the crime bosses that were here earlier.

We left through a window, with Jay climbing out first, and he kept watch while I climbed out myself.

"Okay, Delilah. Call me if you need anything. I'll be in touch.

We'll figure something out to stop whatever's happening in Paris. I know we will." Jay whispered as we snuck past a security camera.

"Alright. I'll be in touch, too." I replied, nodding.

Jay looked at me, one last time, and said, "The world is a dangerous place, Delilah. Don't forget that. There are people, bad people, who don't think like you do. They don't care like I do. Please, *please*, be careful. Promise me."

His plea was so genuine, so raw, I actually stepped forward and hugged him.

He wrapped his arms around me, and I felt a sense of security and belonging in his hold.

He hugged me tightly, and I couldn't help but marvel at how natural it felt, as if I were meant to be there, in that moment, with him. "I promise." I said, still hugging him.

We stayed that way for what could have been seconds or hours, I don't really know.

What I do know is that neither of us wanted to leave, but we knew that eventually we would have to.

Jay and I released our hold at the same time, and he stayed staring at me in that deep way I was growing accustomed to.

"Don't forget me." He said, smiling.

I laughed softly before replying, "I won't."

And with that, Jay turned and disappeared, lost in the darkness as he left me on his way to wherever he was going.

My internal clock kicked back in, and I knew I had 1 minute to get where I needed to be.

I absently placed my hand over my pocket where the compact lay, and I turned and jogged back to meet with Roy and Scarlet.

Chapter Twenty

The school days came and went, filled with new adventures.

For example, the field ops in CFRC (we had to tail a man in a parka and find out if he was a Winter Texan or not), the experiments in Chemistry (who knew you could turn an apple into liquid form in just 5 minutes?), and a test grade in LCW (the second we entered the room to the second we left, we *had* to speak the African Bantu language).

What I really enjoyed was the warm moments at home I spent with Roy and my parents, complete with hot chocolate and lots of blankets.

Occasionally, when my homework was done and Roy had free time, we would venture down to the garage, which actually doubled as a training room for the whole family.

There, Roy and I would have archery and sparring practice, keeping score of who won what and when.

I always beat Roy in archery, and he always beat me in sparring.

It was just the way nature intended it to be.

I loved having a bow in my hands, the adrenaline as you drew an arrow, and the rush of anticipation as you fired, waiting to see if you hit your mark.

Roy always mocked me, calling me Robin Hood and telling me I should be the next Green Arrow, who he knew was one of my favorite superheroes.

I would mock him back while we were sparring, telling him that he should quit spying and be a martial arts teacher, so that he could create more mini versions of him and create a crime fighting society.

We would laugh, tease, and joke during these sessions, and I hated when they had to come to an end.

I still hadn't told Roy about helping Jay with the Paris op, even though it had been a full 2 weeks since it had happened.

It was the longest I had ever gone without telling him something.

Roy was aware of the op himself, and we were helping each other in putting the pieces together.

We got along well, even if he didn't know I was receiving some outside help.

I had confided in my mom, telling her everything, and asking for advice.

She was proud of me, and unlike Roy, thought that I had made the right decision.

When I had described Jay to her and told her his name, a certain look crossed her face, one that I can't quite name.

It quickly passed and she went back to listening, so I didn't question it.

She was 100% on board with helping me.

I was grateful for her understanding, and it felt like a weight had been lifted from my shoulders.

Knowing that my mom was looking into it as well made me feel so much better.

Jay and I talked every so often, usually to update each other on anything we learned or any leads we found.

The compact allowed me to have visual conversations with him, due to the small camera that was inside.

Sometimes when we were in a rush, it was just a voice call.

Nevertheless, I enjoyed talking to him, and I enjoyed the feeling I got when the compact vibrated and I knew it was him.

I was able to fiddle with my gift and found a variety of features, just as Jay had talked about.

Not only could I call Jay, I could track him as well.

His location fluctuated between Indiana and Minnesota, never staying long enough for a pattern to be picked up.

I figured that since I could track him, he could track me, but I was fine him knowing I was in Texas.

I lived a town full of spies; I'm pretty sure I was safe.

Besides, I trusted Jay, just like he trusted me.

Not only could I use it as a tracking device, but I could use it just like my HoloWatch, from searching the Internet to scanning an item, the compact did it all.

I could message Jay as well, our conversations saved in the airtight security algorithms on each of our devices.

Time went by as Jay and I had our conversations, and we both delved deeper and deeper into figuring out what was planned for Paris.

I couldn't help but feel like we were growing closer and closer with each conversation; sometimes it was strictly mission related, other times we branched out to other aspects of our lives.

I never revealed too much, and neither did he. It was the odd relationship between spy and thief, two people from different worlds, collaborating to reach a common goal.

It got to the point where Jay would just ask how I was doing, genuinely concerned with my well-being.

We would joke, laugh, and talk, like old pen pals reunited.

I genuinely enjoyed having Jay in my life, even if it was a bit unconventional.

I was in my room, working on AP World History homework, when Jay called.

I involuntarily reached up to fix my hair, which I instantly thought was silly.

I smoothed it down anyway, and flipped open the vibrating compact.

Jay's face popped up on screen, his face flushed and sweaty. A towel hung around his neck, and he was sitting in a chair.

"Hey." I greeted him with a smile.

"Hey, yourself." Jay replied, returning my smile.

"You're the one who called me." I said playfully.

"How right you are. Listen, I got some inside information about when all of this might happen. The day after Christmas, December 26." Jay informed me with the first solid, crucial piece of intel either of us had come across.

Up until that point, we had only been theorizing potential dates, theories, and groups who may have been behind the Paris op.

All thoughts of the Agricultural Revolution fled my mind as I absorbed what he relayed to me.

I leaned forward, grasping the compact in my hands.

"Really? How did you find out?" I asked curiously.

Jay smiled slyly before replying, "You have your sources, I have mine."

I cocked my head and said, "Haha, you're so charming. Seriously, who told you about this?"

Jay got up from his chair and walked into what appeared to be a kitchen, where he slid his towel off of his neck and wiped his face.

He looked at the screen thoughtfully, and paused before

saying, "You know, you're cute when you're curious."

He caught me off guard, and I blushed. I laughed nervously and replied, "I'm serious. If you got this info, maybe you can get more."

It was Jay's turn to laugh before responding, "It's not that simple Delilah. A thief has their sources, but they only go so far. I can't just go around with a badge and ask for intel."

I bit my lip and told him, "Gee, don't sugarcoat it so much."

Jay looked at me apologetically and said, "Sorry. It's been a rough few days. Getting that information wasn't as easy as you might think."

It was only when he set down his pocket tablet, turned and walked away from the camera did I notice the dark purple spot on his lower left jaw.

My heart skipped a beat as I took in the image.

"What's that?" I asked cautiously.

Jay glanced at me and continued pouring the glass of orange juice he had set on a table and asked, "What's what?"

I bit my lip before saying, "You know very well what's what. What happened to your cheek?"

Jay took a nice, long drink form his glass before replying, "I told you. Getting that intel wasn't easy."

I blinked. "So you got punched in the face for snooping around? Jay, why didn't you tell me?" I asked, both concerned and incredulous.

Jay rubbed his cheek where the bruise was before replying, "I didn't want you to worry. And for the record, I wasn't punched. I was shoved. Into a metal beam."

I sighed, having learned over the last two weeks that it was best not to argue with Jay. He was like me: stubborn and set in his ways.

"Okay, I'll cross reference the date with my records and see if I can find out who's going to be in Paris for Christmas." I said, relaying my plan.

Jay nodded, "Sounds good. I'll try and see if I can dig up anything else-"

"Oh, no. You're not getting hurt again. If you have to go looking for details, then just be more careful." I cut him off, my tone harsh, yet concerned.

Jay was quiet for a moment, before nodding and replying, "That's fair. As long as you keep your promise of being careful yourself. I wouldn't want a hypocrite as a partner." He smiled to show that he was being playful, but I knew he would hold me to my promise.

"Is it wrong to worry after seeing your friend with a *bruise* on his face?" I countered.

"I didn't say that. I just want you to be careful. You know that." He replied, setting the towel around his neck again.

"You just finished your run?" I asked, changing the subject.

Jay nodded, taking another drink from his glass.

"I ran a little extra today, I needed to clear my head." He said, his voice slightly raw from the ice cold juice he just drank.

"And by 'a little extra', you actually mean…" I prodded.

Jay looked at me, as if unsure what I would think, before saying, "Three miles."

I raised an eyebrow and nodded approvingly, "Impressive."

Jay smiled and finished off his glass of juice, happy that I didn't chew him out for pushing himself too hard.

Jay must have spotted the 8 books piled on top of my desk, because he asked, "How long have you been working on assignments?"

I fiddled with my pencil before replying, "4 hours."

"And when was the last time you took a break?" He prompted.

My silence must have given him the answer, because he stared at me, exasperated.

"I swear, Delilah, you're going to run yourself to the ground. Take a break, or you're going to pass out from exhaustion." Jay scolded.

"I'm taking a break to talk to you, aren't I?" I countered.

Jay gave me a bored look and replied, "You know this doesn't count."

I sighed. A break did sound pretty good…

"Okay, okay. I'll take 10 minutes off." I offered.

Jay raised an eyebrow.

"15?" I asked.

He narrowed his eyes.

"20?" I pleaded.

He crossed his arms.

I huffed, "What do you want from me?" I asked exasperated.

Jay wiped his face again with his towel and replied, "45 minutes, no work, no research, just unwinding. Then I'll be happy."

I blinked. 45 minutes. Almost an hour of time I could be working, wasted instead.

I opened my mouth to speak, when Jay cut me off.

"Don't even try to argue with me, Delilah. I'm not easily ignored." He smiled, and I fought the urge to swoon, not only at his good looks, but at his genuine concern for me.

I sighed. "Alright, 45 minutes. I'll start after I finish this World History assignment."
Jay opened his mouth to say something, but it was my turn to cut him off.

"Don't even try to argue with me. I can be very stubborn." I smiled at my cleverness.

Jay smiled and shook his head, saying, "You're incredible, you know that?"

I blushed and replied, "So are you."

Jay glanced at something across the room, my guess is that it was a clock, and his expression changed as he saw what time it was.

"I gotta run." Jay said, a sadness in his voice that he had to say goodbye.

"Didn't you already have your run?" I teased.

Jay smiled before he could stop himself, and he tried his best to look serious as he said, "Haha, so funny. You know, if this spy thing doesn't work out, you could be a comedian."

I smiled and said, "I'll consider it."

Jay looked at me, somewhat longingly, and said, "See you later, Delilah."

"See you." I said my goodbye, and we both hung up, somewhat unwillingly.

I leaned back in my chair, and took a deep breath.

We had a date to work with.

Whoever was planning this, they were going to strike the day after Christmas.

Paris would be packed with tourists and visitors, the perfect time for something to occur.

I pulled out my laptop and began to cross reference known criminals and their location plans with the date of December 26.

Once I had the algorithm up and running, I turned back to my World History homework, and heard Jay's voice in my head.

I sighed, pushed myself away from my desk back on my rolling chair, and stood.

I spent the next 45 minutes listening to music and practicing shooting with my bow.

Whatever people may have thought, it helped me unwind.
I was about to pick an arrow from the quiver on my back when Roy walked into the training room where I was.

"There you are. I went to your room, but you weren't there. Kind of odd that I find you here rather than doing homework, don't you think?" He asked coyly, in his big brother way.

I drew back my bow and aimed at the bull's eye across the room from where I stood.

I took a breath, and fired, hitting my mark perfectly on the black dot in the middle of the bull's eye.

"Just wanted to take a break, that's all." I said coolly, while walking over to the target to retrieve my arrow.

Roy stayed staring at me, in mock disbelief. He even had his jaw hung open before he said, "Who are you and what have you done with my sister?"

I rolled my eyes and softly punched him in the shoulder, and he laughed.

"So have you figured anything out about our Paris dilemma?" Roy asked, biting into an apple he had brought along.

"Actually, I came across some intel that I think could really help us out. I got the date of the event." I told him.

Roy stopped mid-bite and looked at me.

"No way, how?" He asked, getting excited.

"I have my ways... Anyhow, I have an algorithm that's currently running through criminals and their known location plans, compiling a list of who will be in Paris at the time of... Whatever is going to happen." I told him, quickly changing the subject.

Roy nodded and took a bite of his apple before saying, "Great job, Runt. Once we have that list, we can dig deeper until we find motives, details, and eventually, our perps. I'll go check on the email inboxes, voicemails and such to see if we've found anything."

Scarlet had the brilliant idea to hack into known big bad criminals' emails and cell phone logs, keeping track of who said what, where, when, and how.

We had all been checking periodically, hoping to find the one clue that would explain everything.

Scarlet knew about Jay being in on the op, and she could not have been happier.

Once, Jay called me while I was with her, and she couldn't help but sneak a peek at him.

"I've got four letters for you, Miss Verdant," she had said, "C. U. T. E. You better catch that one and not let him go."

I had been grateful for Jay not hearing Scarlet's verdict of his looks, and I couldn't help but laugh.

I nodded at Roy and told him, "Sounds good. I'll tell you if I come across anything."

Roy smiled, took one last bite of his apple, and set it down on a table, saying, "I know you will."

I felt a pang of guilt stab me in the chest, and I managed to smile weakly before he left.

I knew I was going to have to tell him sometime; I couldn't keep the fact that I was working with Jay away from him forever.

I closed my eyes and took a deep breath.

I drew back my bow and fired at a different target this time.

The arrow flew through the air and hit its mark perfectly.

I took off my quiver and set my bow back on its rack as I headed out the door.

I left the room and the apple pinned to the wall with my arrow.

What I didn't leave was my concern and worry for everything that was going to happen.

My mom had called to announce that she was going to be later than usual in getting home, so Roy and I were getting dinner ready for her.

My dad had come home on schedule, but we refused to let him in the kitchen to help.

Don't get me wrong, I love my dad to pieces.

His cooking is another story.

The one food he could possible "cook" without causing a fire would have to be popcorn, and even then he needs to stay and keep watch so it doesn't burn.

While my dad showered and we cooked, Roy's HoloWatch beeped in the middle of him taking rolls out of the oven.

"What's that for?" I asked as I stirred a pot of macaroni and cheese.

Roy smiled at me, a twinkle in his eyes.

"That, my dear sister, is an alert telling me we found something in the emails and call logs." Roy explained, smiling the whole time.

I grinned, and even jumped a little.

Roy took out the rolls and covered them in foil.

From there, he dashed to his room to check on the alert.

I breathed a sigh of relief.

I had gotten a list of criminals who would be in Paris on the 26th, and I had to admit, the list was a lot longer than I wanted it to be.

Narrowing it down would be harder than I had hoped.

I cooked the chicken slices in a pan, and finished boiling the macaroni by the time Roy came back in.

"Well?" I asked in anticipation, "What did you find?"

Roy got back to buttering the rolls, purposely putting me in suspense.

Roy pretended not to hear me, and he glanced at me through the corner of his eye, "Hm? Did you say something?"

I poked him with the side of a fork that *wasn't* sharp and he laughed.

"Okay, okay. I got a name of a Corporation. Spades Enterprises." He revealed.

I let his information sink in, my mind racing as I put different pieces of the puzzle together.

Spades Enterprises was an international corporation that specialized in technology and stock markets. They had an iron grip on many countries' economies, bringing in a lot of revenue from several companies and governments.

What the world didn't know, was that Spades Enterprises was also one of the most prominent (and not to mention way, *way*, underground) arms and weapons dealers.

The CEO, Xavier Bêche, was known worldwide as the man who helps enrich children's education by providing technology advancements to schools and children centers.

He was also known underground for his weapons dealing business, but O.U.O never had enough evidence against him to do anything about it.

He was also a good friend and associate of Jacque Mazder, the man from the meeting.

Things were starting to look up.

I voiced my opinion to Roy, and he agreed 100%.

We told my dad about our findings, and he was impressed with our work.

Roy and I had told my parents at the same time, but it wasn't until later that I told my mom about Jay.

There wasn't a doubt in my mind that she had already told my dad, but he wasn't acting any differently towards me.

Spy skills was what I believed.

My mom came home shortly after, hungry and happy to see dinner ready.

Roy and I told her about what we found out, and she was pleased with our work.

We all discussed potential plans to investigate further, and once dinner was over, I headed to my room to call Jay.

On my way, I was stopped by my mom grabbing my hand as I went up the stairs.

I took in the look on her face, and I knew what was coming before she said it.

"I think now is a good time to tell him, sweetie. You've had your first big break in the case, after all. Now is a good time." My mother gave me her advice in the most motherly tone possible.

I bit my lip, nervous for what came next.

I knew she was right.

I had to tell Roy about Jay.

The only issue then would be whether or not I would be alive to see the Paris op pull through.

I sighed, and promised myself that I would tell Roy as soon as it was just me and him.

Tomorrow was Saturday; it would be just my brother and I inside of the house.

I would tell him then, and everything would go fine.

Right?

Chapter Twenty One

*L*ater that night, after I got my homework finished, I was so tired and worn that, for a moment, I was completely oblivious of the time.

I picked up my compact and called Jay, eager to tell him about what Roy and I had figured out.

It wasn't until he answered that I realized how late it was.

Luckily, Jay was still awake like me.

"Hey, Delilah. What's up?" He asked, his voiced tinged with drowsiness.

It was the single cutest thing I had ever heard.

I could tell he was trying to fall asleep, but he wasn't able to; it was very apparent in his voice.

"I have news." I enticed, my own voice sounding not-so-wide-awake.

"News at 2:30 in the morning… That's the best kind of news." He joked.

"Sorry, I didn't realize how late it was." I apologized.

"No worries, I like hearing your voice." He replied smoothly.

I blushed, trying to hide my smile.

"So, like I said, I have news. I think we figured out who's going to be behind the Paris op." I told him.

Jay leaned forward, hazel eyes sparkling.

"Really? Who?" He asked, anticipation building.

"Xavier Bêche," I explained, "CEO of-"

"Spades Enterprises," Jay continued, "Also, head of an underground-"

"Weapons dealing enterprise." I finished for him.

I expected him to at least be happy that we had a solid lead to whom was behind the Paris op.

I guess it's safe to say the he *wasn't* happy.

His whole demeanor fell, and he sighed deeply.

"Bêche. It had to be Xavier Bêche." He said in a low voice, rubbing his hazel eyes.

"How did you find out that he was a candidate?" He asked.

"We had a database that held potential suspects' emails, call logs, and messages. We found an email from Spades Enterprises, talking about the 'event' occurring in Paris, and was voicing that all of the 'supplies' were ready for use. I double checked that Xavier was going to be there on the 26th, and I found out that he had already booked a hotel there for when he arrived." I explained to Jay.

Jay nodded, lost in thought for a moment.

"What?" I asked, curious towards his reaction.

Jay shook his head, before replying, "I know Bêche. I've met him multiple times. Let's just say... He's not very fond of me."

I wrinkled my brow, confused, "Not fond of you, how? Why?" I asked.

Jay let out a sigh before saying, "Let's just say that once, I took his car in an emergency, and he wasn't very understanding, even though I returned it."

My eyes went wide.

"You *stole* Xavier Bêche's *car?*" I asked as loud as I dared.

My family was asleep, after all.

Jay pressed his lips together before saying, "*Stole* has a very negative connotation, don't you think? And besides, I didn't steal it. I borrowed it, and gave it back. I fixed the ding, so he didn't even notice..."

"Oh, geez, Jay." It was my turn to lean back in my chair and rub my eyes.

"Do I even want to know what you were doing with his car?"

I asked.

"Well, the story involves a bag of my money, an art thief, and a car chase. Is that enough for you to paint a picture?" He asked.

I nodded, replying, "Yeah, I got the picture."

Jay shook his head, still unable to get over the fact that it was Xavier Bêche who was probably behind everything.

"Well, we still don't know for sure. We need to plan something to make absolutely certain that it's him." I assured.

Jay nodded, running a hand through his hair, making it even more adorably messy.

"I'll see if I can get back on his good side, and I'll work on trying to find a good day to break into his main headquarters to see what we can find." Jay voiced his plan.

I raised an eyebrow, "Is there really a 'good' day to break into a world renowned technology and weapon tycoon's headquarters?" I teased.

"Yes, Delilah, there is. Trust me, I've gone on bad days." He replied.

My suspicions were raised, but I figured I was better off not trying to pry it out of him.

I smiled, and yawned involuntarily.

I covered my mouth and closed my eyes, leaning back in my chair.

"Get some sleep, Delilah. Don't think I can't see those books on your desk. Get some rest." He said, tired as well.

"In that case, you get some sleep yourself. I'm not the only one who's tired." I told him.

Jay smiled, and his hazel eyes made me want to melt.

"If I could sleep, I would. I've been lying in bed for hours, *trying* to sleep." He confessed.

"Well, what's wrong?" I asked.

Jay rubbed his eyes, and shook his head, shifting positions in his bed.

"Nothing for you to be worried about, Delilah." He said to me, having my best interest in mind.

I bit my lip, and eventually said, "Alright. Just promise me you'll get *some* sleep, okay?"

Jay smiled and nodded, and replied, "I'll ask you to do the same thing. Deal?"

I smiled, "Deal."

Jay smiled sleepily, and added, "But, don't go just yet. I like knowing I can talk to you."

I smiled, and replied, "I like it, too."

Jay shifted positions in bed again, and he set his pocket tablet down on what I figured was a table.

I went through my homework, making sure I hadn't missed anything, and double checking answers I was wary of.

Once I thought Jay was asleep, I heard his voice.

"Delilah?" He asked, groggily.

My heart fluttered, and I knew he was half asleep.

"Yeah?" I answered.

"Thank you." He said, his voice becoming softer.

"For what?" I asked, surprised.

He replied, "Knowing what I am, and deciding to stay anyway."

I was shocked; I hadn't been expecting anything like that.

Being a spy, I could relate to how Jay felt: when you live a life in the shadows, constantly being hidden and changing your cover, it's rare to find someone who knows what's behind the cover, and accepts what they find.

Some people prefer the cover.

"Thank you, too." I told him.

"For what?" He asked, still sleepy.

"The exact same thing." I replied, simply.

Jay stirred, and said, "You're not a thief. You don't have anything to hide." His voice grew more and more faint with every word.

And with that, he fell asleep, leaving me to ponder his statement.

Morning came, and I awoke with the awareness that I was going to have to tell Roy about Jay.

I sighed, tossed off the covers, and made my way through my morning routine.

After getting dressed, taming my hair, and brushing my teeth, I found my parents getting ready to head out the door to their jobs.

I hugged them both goodbye, and when they left, I felt the pressure build.

Roy must have sensed that something was going on with me, because he came up and put a hand on my shoulder.

"What's up?" He asked, genuinely concerned.

I took a deep breath, and dived right in.

"I have something to tell you." I said warily.

Roy grew wary himself, and replied, "Alright... Let's talk then."

We walked into the living room, and I sat on the couch while he took his spot on the recliner.

"What's wrong? You're so nervous." He voiced his opinion.

"That's because I have an idea of what's coming, and I'm not looking forward to it." I replied.

Roy leaned back in his recliner, and he gestured for me to start.

"Okay. You know how we went to that meeting in Detroit two weeks ago?" I asked.

Roy nodded.

"Well, we weren't the only ones there to get some information." I admitted.

Roy's expression grew wary, but he listened as I told him everything, from Jay at the factory to me telling him about Xavier Bêche.

I waited for his reaction, and honestly, the longer I waited, the more scared I became.

"Say something, please." I said, eager to get the yelling over with.

Roy blinked, and rubbed the side of jaw.

I inhaled sharply; that was a sign that he was mad.

Like, *really* mad.

Roy leaned forward, and looked at me, saying, "I can't believe it. You're working with a thief."

"Roy, it's not that simple-" I started.

"Yeah, I think it *is* that simple. You're working with a *thief!* You've allowed yourself to trust someone that we hunt down as our *jobs*. Do you realize, truly realize, what you're doing? You don't anything about him! For all we know, this is just a rouse to get us cornered. How can you trust someone you just met?! And don't even try to throw that 'he's different' excuse at me. I can't believe you've been keeping communication with a *criminal*. A *criminal,* Kay! How could you make that kind of judgement call?!" He scolded me harshly.

I bit my lip, biting my tongue so that I didn't say anything that would only make him angrier.

I kept my own annoyance and anger under wraps, and waited to calmly get my input in.

"You said it yourself. I make good judgement calls. Jay has helped getting certain information on this op, and he's not a bad guy. He's not like other thieves-"

Roy cut me off, saying, "There's no such thing. All thieves are the same. They lie, cheat, and steal. There's no in between."

I bit my lip, and slowly continued, "How would you know? You're always set in the way things are. You don't allow leeway."

"Leeway? Are you kidding? That's your argument? Kay, he's a *thief.* He's told you so himself! He's from the other side of the law, do you understand that? Do you, really? I can't believe..." He trailed off, as if a thought dawned on him.

"No." He shook his head, "No. I'm not going to let that happen."

I was genuinely confused, asking, "Let what happen?"

Roy looked me straight in the face, and his blue eyes were hard and cold, like ice.

My green eyes must have had a despair to them, because his softened, although his tone didn't.

"I'm not going to let my baby sister fall for a low life crook. I won't. You made this call, and I don't agree. Not at all. It hurts that you waited this long to tell me. That only fuels my decision. I am *not* going to let you fall for a thief like him." He said harshly and assertively.

I was taken aback.

Whatever Roy was going to say, I sure wasn't expecting that.

"I-" I started, but Roy cut me off again.

"He just likes the thrill of knowing he's doing something other thieves don't get to do. He's flirting with danger. Think about it. He's a thief, partnered with a spy. Do you know how insane that is? He's working *with* a spy! Learning how we work, what we do, how we get things done. He knows that side of you, he knows the most secret side of you!" He exclaimed.

It got to the point where I was tearing up, and trying my hardest not to let my tears spill over.

I took a deep breath and said, as assertively as I could, "You don't get it. He doesn't see the spy. He sees me!"

Roy looked at me deeply, and I knew he was thinking that this was one of the defining moments in sibling relationships.

Roy swallowed, and said, "I'm not letting this happen. I'm sorry. Work with him, be his partner until the op is over. After that, no."

Roy stood up and left the room, leaving me hurting.

I bit my lip, stood and went straight to the training room, where I beat my frustration into an innocent manikin.

This road bump would only add to the worry and pressure.

The weekend came and went, and being back at school was a relief.

I don't have to deal with Roy and his disapproval, I could just sit back and learn.

When I wasn't in school, I spent a lot of time at Jerry D's, trying to avoid Roy and his disapproval as much as possible.

Jerry immediately picked up that something was wrong, since Roy wasn't with me, but he never goaded as much as he could have.

He told me stories, and I helped him clean up the shop after I ate.

That's how my routine went for the next two weeks, wake up, go to school, go to Jerry D's, come home, do homework, do it all over again the next day.

Jay called me periodically, and I enjoyed having him there, even though Roy greatly disapproved.

Jay immediately saw that something was up with me, and he tried getting it out of me.

"Nothing for you to be worried about." I told him.

I could tell Jay was concerned, but he respected the fact that I didn't want to talk about it.

Jay gave me the location of Xavier Bêche's main headquarters in southern France, and we conspired when to meet up and break in.

I talked to Scarlet and my parents about it, when the bomb was dropped.

My parents were called away on a mission in Buenos Aires, and they wouldn't be able to help with the Paris op.

My heart dropped.

I had been counting on my parents giving reinforcement during the mission, but all hope of that was lost.

Roy and I had told O.U.O during the debriefing after the factory meeting that there was potentially something happening in France.

O.U.O had left it in our hands, and were giving us the necessary resources to complete our mission (how else would we have gotten access to the emails?).

Although my parents leaving was a setback, at least I had Roy, Scarlet, and Jay.

Scarlet's parents were originally going to help, but they got sent on a mission to Tokyo the week before, and I doubted they could make it.

It saddened me that we wouldn't get to be spending Christmas with our parents, but that's the life we lived.

We didn't get a say in it.

On the first weekend after school let out, Roy, Scarlet and I set out to meet Jay in France.

We landed, threw our things in the hotel room, and met up with Jay outside at a table.

Jay was sitting with what seemed to be a sketch pad in front of him, and when he saw me, he closed the book and stood up in one motion.

"Hey, Delilah." He smiled, and the sun caused his tan skin to glow, making me want to swoon.

"Hey, there." I replied, smiling as I walked up to him.

"It's good to see you, right here, in front of me." He said smoothly, his hazel eyes warm as he took me in.

"I could say the same thing about you." I replied, my smile never leaving me.

Scarlet walked up after me, and raised an eyebrow at Jay.

She extended her hand out towards him, and he shook her hand.

"Hi, I'm Scarlet, her best friend, but I'm sure you knew that." Scarlet smiled at Jay, analyzing him from his leather jacket to his brown suede boots.

"I did, in fact. I'm Jay, although I'm sure you knew that." He replied, smiling at Scarlet, and then me.

Oh, when he smiled at me.

Roy walked up then, and gave Jay a cold look.

"Good to see you, again." Jay said, trying to play tough guy.

"I'm sure it is." Roy replied, keeping up with the harsh looks.

Jay looked from Roy to me, and sat back down.

There were four chairs at the square table, and we each took one.

I sat across from Jay, with Scarlet on my left and Roy on my right.

"Okay. What do you have?" I asked Jay.

Jay reached down into his slim backpack and slipped in the sketch pad. He pulled out a folder, and laid it on the table.

"The main building is located 7 miles from here, and I know Xavier is in town right now, which means his office is in use. I managed to get my hands on his schedule, and I know key time frames where he won't be there, and when security is the least tight. From there, we can plan when to go in, how we're getting in, and what we're looking for." Jay explained coolly, calmly, and was very collected.

I had to stop myself from swooning.

Scarlet and I stole a glance, and the look on her face made me want to bury my face in my hands and never look up.

She smiled at me mischievously, and it took all of my willpower not to kick her from under the table.

"Alright, knowing that, we can schedule our plan and have everything sketched out before we go in. I got building schematics that I accessed from a database, and I managed to map out 5 different routes we can go in through." I said, ignoring Scarlet's looks.

Jay leaned back in his chair and smiled slyly, "And by 'accessed' you mean…" He prompted.

"Fine. I hacked." I admitted.

Jay smiled and nodded, approving of my honesty.

I could feel Roy tense at my side, our sibling telepathy alerting me to his feelings.

I tried my best to ignore him and went back to planning.

"So, if we have the schematics and other details, when is the soonest time we can go in?" Scarlet asked, eager to get the action part of the mission started.

Jay leaned forward, looking at his self-compiled game plan.

"Bêche will be there all day today, all hours. It's not until tomorrow that he arrives at 6 am, and leaves at 12 pm so that he could fly to Paris. That would be the key day, since all of the employees will be scrambling with his departure." Jay answered.

Scarlet nodded, saying, "We're all going to need comms," and looked at me for my opinion.

I nodded and mulled it over, before asking, "Do you think we have time to plan by tomorrow night, Roy?"

Roy hadn't said a word since he had sat down, and it was only when I addressed him that he leaned forward, saying, "If we start planning now, we can get everything together by the time he leaves tomorrow at noon. After that, we can stay observing the building in case plans change, and we'll go in when the time is right."

I nodded, agreeing with him on the plan.

Jay nodded as well, and he looked at me.

"Alright," I said, meeting his gaze, "Let's get started."

Chapter Twenty Two

*A*fter a long night of planning in our hotel room, with quick trips to a nearby café for hot chocolate, coffee, and baguettes, we were all worn out by exhaustion and jet lag.

I decided to leave the hotel room and clear my head, so I found myself outside on the balcony of the 4th story, leaning over a railing at 5 am, without a jacket.

Sometimes I questioned my logic.

I looked out into the sky, where the last stars of night twinkled high above me.

I found myself lost in thought as I watched the stars above me, and I was actually surprised when I had a guest join me outside.

"You alright?" Jay asked, coming up beside me, hands in the pocket of his leather jacket.

I nodded, continuing watching the sky.

"Yeah, I'm just thinking." I answered honestly.

"Can I ask what about?" He said, leaning over the railing and taking a step closer to me.

I sighed before replying, "Everything. This, our mission. Home, my parents. You."

Jay seemed surprised that I mentioned him, and he asked, "What about me?"

I glanced at him, and said, "To be honest, I don't really know. Every time I see you, it's something different. I find it odd that two people so different could get along as well as we do. And then again, we don't even know that much about each other."

Jay stepped closer to me, his hands leaving his pockets.

"I know enough." Jay replied, taking my hands in his.

His warm hands encasing my freezing fingers caused me to shiver, and his grip on my hands tightened.

"You're cold." He said, taking off his jacket.

I shook my head, saying, "No, keep it. I don't want you to be cold because of me."

Jay gave me a look and said, "I was born and raised in Minnesota, and I'm an Indiana local. I can handle a little cold, Miss South Texas."

He draped his jacket over my shoulders, and the warmth felt amazing.

I pulled it tighter around me, and gave a half laugh.

"I bet you do this to all the girls." I joked.

Jay shook his head, stepping closer to me.

"No," he spoke softly, "You're the first. Just you."

He left one hand on the railing, and the other hand found my right cheek, as he leaned in slowly.

My heart fluttered and pounded against my chest, like a butterfly trying to break free.

I closed my eyes, leaning in as well, savoring this perfect moment.

Until I heard Scarlet's voice in my ear, saying, "Guys, come back inside. It's almost time to leave."

Jay and I both froze at the sound, being shocked out of the magical moment we had been in only seconds before.

His face was dangerously close to my own, and my heart couldn't help but beat faster.

We stayed that way for a moment, close.

Eventually, Jay pulled away, and he put both of his hands in the pockets of his jeans.

"We should go. Don't want to keep them waiting." He said with a weak smile.

I didn't want to go.

I wanted to go back to that perfect moment, where there were no problems, just Jay and I in our own little world.

I could see it in Jay's eyes that he felt the same way.

I smiled back, and slipped his jacket off of my shoulders.

I handed it back, and headed back into the hotel room, heart still pounding.

We had packed up and headed out the door at 5:45 am, and we were discreetly watching the headquarters for any sign of Xavier Bêche.

We watched as he entered the building, and continued observing the hustle and bustle of the headquarters.

Roy was directly across the street, watching from a bench.

Scarlet was to the right, leaning against a lamp post.

Jay and I were on separate roof tops, watching from above.

I had asked Jay if he had managed to get on Xavier's good side, and his answer was a resounding "no."

We just had to settle for watching the building.

We had organized gear and finalized our plan the night before, so now it was just a matter of watching the headquarters and making sure nothing went wrong.

Hours passed with nothing interesting occurring, and we each took quick breaks to run to a café one block away for a drink and some food.

The buzz of French speakers was constant down below, and I loved knowing that there was constant movement, it wasn't just us sitting and waiting while nothing was happening.

Eventually, Xavier stepped out of the building, clad in a suit so formal I had to wonder if he had just left a model's photo shoot, and walked up to his car.

He slid inside and drove away, in the direction of particularly luxurious and expensive residences.

While searching his house would have been smart, it wouldn't have done us much good.

Jay had explained that Xavier was the kind of person to keep all of his work related things in one place: at work.

Searching his home wouldn't do us any good.

We continued to wait as the day went on, and at around 6:00 pm, we all headed back to the hotel to get suited up for the break in.

The next few hours until midnight were a blur of triple-checking gear, memorizing the schematics, going over our plan, and memorizing the schedule of the security guards and their cycles.

By the time it was 11:45 pm, we were all dressed, geared up, and were on the rooftop of Spades Enterprises.

"Um, are the windows *supposed* to be under lockdown like that?" Scarlet asked, the slightest bit concerned.

"No, they aren't. Bêche must have gotten extra paranoid and issued extra protocols, since he wouldn't be in town." Jay replied, pressing his lips together.

"Great. There goes 3 out of 5 of our secure entry points." Scarlet said, slightly annoyed.

Roy held a pair of binoculars to his face as he looked down below, "Make it 4. A security guard just walked out by the east door. All of us sneaking past a security camera is doable. All of us sneaking past a security guard… I don't like those odds."

I walked over to a certain part of the roof, and said, "Well, we still have one option."

Roy looked over to where I was standing, and said, "We can't *all* go in through there, Runt."

"Who said we all would? Besides, it's our only entry at this point. I'm small enough to fit." I replied.

Roy thought about it, and turned to Scarlet.

Scarlet shrugged, "She's right. It's our only way in. I would go but…" she shuddered, "dust and spiders. So many spiders."

I crossed my arms and cocked my hip, giving Roy a, 'I Told You So' kind of look.

Roy sighed and checked the clock, finally saying, "Fine. But be careful. Keep your comms on automatic, and no, I repeat, *no* unnecessary risks. Am I clear?"

"As crystal." I replied, nodding.

"Alright, then. Go grab the climbing gear." Roy instructed.

I walked over to the corner of the roof with our bags, and I grabbed the climbing gear and attached it to my utility belt.

Jay walked up, telling me in a low voice, "Be careful, okay? If you got caught…" Jay trailed off, as if not wanting to think about his statement.

I looked into his gaze and said, "I'll be okay."

Jay nodded, and we walked back to join Scarlet and Roy together.

My internal clock told me it was 11:59, and I could tell Roy knew as well.

"Ready?" Roy asked, genuine concern in his eyes.

"Ready." I replied.

He disabled security features of the building on his HoloWatch, and pulled off the metal covering to the air conditioning shaft.

I climbed inside and began the trek to Xavier Bêche's Tech Lab to fulfill our plan.

Like a rain drop on velvet, I silently dropped from a dusty air-shaft to the floor of Spades Enterprises, clad in navy and shrouded in the dark.

I glanced around the Tech Lab I had landed in, knowing that a door was 32 ft. to my left, thanks to the building blueprints I had memorized 16 hours earlier.

Almost subconsciously, I began to carry out my mission, silently gliding across to the floor to the main computer at the back of the lab.

I unclipped a mini-flashlight from my utility belt, shone it on the desktop, and switched on the PC.

While the computer warmed up, I slipped a USB Drive out of my pocket and held it millimeters away from the port I was going to plug it into.

I counted down how much time I had before the left-wing security guard came into the lab for a routine check.

64 seconds.

Plenty of time.

The second the computer's lock screen came up, I plugged in the USB Drive.

I watched expectantly as the screen went from displaying Spade Enterprises' logo to an array of speeding numbers on a green background.

I smiled as the algorithm on the drive unlocked the computer and pilfered through the files, picking out any of particular interest.

While the USB Drive was working its magic, I began to search the drawers for any folders or documents that would provide any vital information.

Oddly, the drawers were filled with pens, paper clips, calculators, and other generic office supplies.

Yet, there were no folders or documents in sight.

I carefully stripped a paper off of a sticky notes pad, folded it, and slipped it into my pocket, as a souvenir.

My internal clock told me that 38 seconds remained before the guard came in, and as if on cue, the computer screen flashed brightly.

The USB Drive had done its job, and I knew that it had copied files and erased any potential digital fingerprints of mine with efficiency.

With 22 seconds left, I had unplugged the USB, turned off the computer and made my way to the airshaft I had popped out from.

I unclipped a rope and hook from my belt, and I threw it up to the shaft.

The hook sailed through the opening, attached to the frame, and I began to pull myself up.

Once I was safely in the shaft, I rolled up my rope and hook and clipped it back onto my belt.

No sooner had I placed the cover of the shaft back onto the opening, the guard opened the door and stepped into the room.

Mission accomplished.

Chapter Twenty Three

"I can't believe this." Roy said, reading through the data files I had extracted.

"I know," Scarlet agreed, "This is…"

"Insane." Jay and I finished for her.

We were all crowded around a laptop, looking through the plans for what Xavier was calling, "The Eiffel Tower Heist".

The plan was that on December 26th, he and several other associates would all gather atop the Eiffel Tower, surveying the scene until rush hour started. From there, multiple different employees around Paris would launch fireworks up into the sky, creating the bait of luring people outside of their businesses to better watch the show in broad daylight.

The fireworks would explode and disperse a sleeping gas that would cause anyone within the vicinity to pass out on the spot. After that, Xavier's men would start ransacking the businesses, taking anything of value and worth. Anyone who tried to defy them, would face severe consequences.

This was crazy.

Mazder had been right when he said it would wreak havoc and cause destruction.

The people would only stay passed out for so long, and when Xavier's men stormed businesses to rob them, imagine the chaos that would ensue after they woke up and found a bunch of armed masked men stealing everything of worth.

The city would be a mess.

When the police couldn't keep up with the mass amount of people running around screaming and the mass amount of masked men, it was only a matter of time before riots began.

I hated to admit it, but the plan was... ingenious.

We all immediately got to work organizing our gear, luggage, and findings, and packing everything up.

We checked out of the hotel and hopped on a train to Paris; we could all agree that we had absolutely no time to waste.

Along the way, we conspired our plan on how we were going to stop it all.

It wasn't going to be easy, we all knew that much.

What we did know, is that we needed a plan, and fast.

Jay stepped away and made a phone call, and upon his return he relayed the news that Bêche would be staying at the largest hotel in Paris, Room 6A, and had already arrived via private jet.

We had a little over a week to foil Xavier's plans, but I would have personally wanted to stop The Eiffel Tower Heist sooner rather than later.

It took 3 days to get to Paris by train, and we used almost every second to come up with our own counter attack.

We would hop on one train to the next, only stopping for a quick bite of food before getting on the next train.

We took shifts organizing data and contributing to the plan, sometimes one person working while the others slept, sometimes one person sleeping while the others worked.

About 20 minutes before we arrived in Paris, I woke up and found myself leaning on Jay's shoulder, where he was asleep as well.

It took a moment before my internal clock kicked in, and I was able to estimate the time before we got off of the train.

"Hey," I whispered, gently nudging Jay on the shoulder.

"Wake up, come on." I urged softly, nudging him harder.

Jay stirred and woke, yawning and asking me sleepily, "We there yet?"

"No, but almost. We have 20 minutes." I replied.

"So I could have had 20 more minutes of blissfully sleep.

What a way to start the day." He said, winking at me to show he was joking.

I spotted Roy walking towards the booth we were sitting at, and he sat down next to Scarlet, who had her eyes closed as she listened to music, but we all knew she wasn't really sleeping.

"Did you come up with anything else?" I asked, stretching as much as I could without accidentally punching Jay in the face.

Roy nodded, nudging his backpack with his shoe.

"I added in a few more details and packed up. We can go over the overall plan once we're at the hotel." Roy explained.

Scarlet groaned and rubbed her neck as she sat up straight, "Remind me again why we travelled by train instead of by plane. We would have been there already," she complained.

I raised an eyebrow at her and replied, "Would you rather have a hotel to stay at, or comfy transportation? O.U.O already got us the plane to tickets to come here, and we have the tickets to go back. They gave us money for transportation, and food. They're paying for the hotel."

Scarlet pouted and muttered, "I hate when logic prevails."

I stood up and stretched some more, involuntarily popping my right shoulder and left knee at the same time.

"Just because it's logical," I said wincing, "doesn't mean I don't agree with you."

I sat back down, and Roy raised an eyebrow at me.

"What? Can't handle a little soreness? No wonder I lasted longer than you during our run in Chicago. You got too sore." Roy goaded.

I held up a finger to protest, "Hey, I had *literally* taken the fall for you the day before, and my ankle was messed up."

Roy rolled his eyes, "Yeah, I remember. I yelled at you for putting yourself in danger like that."

"Some things never change, do they?" I asked.

Roy shook his head, saying, "Nope. And they never will."

Jay turned to Scarlet, and asked, "Do they always try to one-up each other like this?"

"No. Sometimes they just bash each other for the fun of it."

Scarlet replied before putting her earbuds back in.

I was happy that, gradually, Roy and I had gotten back into our normal groove of things.

Yes, he still despised Jay with every fiber in his being, but I caught on that Roy respected him, the same way Jay respected him.

The rest of the train ride was spent discussing where we would go first: dinner, or hotel.

After much deliberation, we headed to the hotel first, threw in our stuff, and then dashed to a café, where we all had our fair share of food and drink.

The clock was still ticking, and once we finished eating, we launched our plan into action.

We would track Xavier from his hotel room to certain places around Paris, until we could figure out where he was meeting with his associates.

From there, we would storm the place and take out as many of his colleagues as we could, gather as much data as we could muster, and confiscate all of their supplies.

It wasn't the most brilliant plan in the world, but since we were pressed for time, it would have to do.

Back at the hotel, I started checking security cameras around the hotel where Xavier was until I managed to see him hop in a cab and take off.

From there, I hopped from one camera to the next, watching where he was going.

At the same time, Roy kept track of any other criminals who may have been Xavier's associates, tracking their every move.

Finally, after hours of spying, we came to the conclusion that they were all converging at a single meeting point: a technology store that sold none other than Spades Electronics.

We all packed up immediately, anxious to get going.

When I thought we were ready to go, Roy stopped me.

"Runt, wait. I've got a surprise for you." Roy grinned and unzipped a particularly bulky portion of his backpack that he hadn't opened since we arrived in France.

I stopped and asked warily, "Okay… What is it?"

Roy's grin turned mischievous as he reached into the pack, and pulled out my bow and fully stocked quiver.

My jaw dropped.

"No way!" I exclaimed, running up to hug him.

"How did you bring these?" I asked, excited.

Roy shrugged, saying, "It was simple. This is a standard O.U.O metal masking backpack. It stretches amazingly, so everything fit."

I hugged him again, and said, "Thank you. Taking down these guys will be a *lot* more fun, now."

Roy hugged me back and smiled.

Jay and Scarlet watched from the door, and Scarlet wore a big smile on her face.

Jay, on the other hand, held a look of sadness, almost longing.

He noticed my looking at him, and he turned away.

I was confused over his expression, but there was no time to think about that.

I packed up my trusty weapon of choice and we headed out the door, focused on the task at hand.

We hailed a cab and tried to enjoy the car ride to the store, each of us suppressing our own anticipation.

Once there, we snuck up to the roof, dodging security cameras and climbing up the back of the building.

"Alright," Roy said, taking the lead, "it's almost night. Something tells me that they're going to be here for a while, and once we have the cover of the dark, we'll sneak in and declare arrest. Am I clear?"

Scarlet nodded, Jay agreed, and I said, "As crystal."

"Good. For now, let's just check our gear and keep an eye out for anyone else who comes in and doesn't come back out. We don't yet know how many people are going to be in there, or where exactly they're meeting. We'll search the rooms when the time comes. Runt, can you find blueprints on this place?" Roy asked.

I pulled up a database on my HoloWatch and replied, "I've

been trying since we found out this was the place. I've come across original designs, but oddly, none official. The only one I did find had an extra room, underground, unlabeled."

Roy thought over what I had relayed to him, and said, "More than likely, that's where they are. We'll check other rooms as we make our way down, but I have a hunch that that's the place we're looking for."

I nodded, and moved to sit against a large metal object bolted to the roof.

Jay came and sat beside me, and we began to go over potential associates of Bêche.

I went through my list of criminals, and Jay confirmed whether or not he knew if they were known to have worked with Xavier before.

We paired that information with whom we knew for a fact was in Paris, and after a while we got our group.

We compiled a list of 11 people, which I showed to Roy.

He went over it, memorizing each name and face, recognizing a few as he looked over the group.

Scarlet looked it over as well, and we all had an idea of who we may have been up against.

Night couldn't have come fast enough, but when it did, we were all prepared.

"Remember, split up and search the whole place; we each have our area. If you find anything, use comms. It's an open frequency, not on manual mode. If nothing comes up, we all meet at the room below ground. No one, and I mean *no one* goes in until we're all there. Got it?" Roy asked.

"Got it." Scarlet, Jay, and I replied in unison.

"Good." Roy replied, "Execute."

From there, we each slipped through a small window on the roof, leading into some kind of office.

Scarlet had already disabled the security functions after office hours, and we were able to slip in without setting anything off.

We silently split up and went towards our assigned areas, Roy taking front, I taking back, Scarlet with left, and Jay with right.

No sooner had Roy and Scarlet split, Jay grabbed my hand.

I put a finger onto my comms unit, temporarily blocking the frequency so the others wouldn't hear me.

"What?" I asked in a low voice.

Jay did the same thing I did with his comms unit, and replied, "Do you really think I'm going to let you roam around in the same building as Xavier Bêche alone?"

His concern warmed my heart, and I smiled at him.

He smiled back, and together we searched both of our assigned areas.

We both came up empty, and told Roy and Scarlet about each of our sides.

"I didn't find anything either, just some seriously sick headphones on sale." Scarlet voiced her own input.

"I came up empty, too. Rendezvous at the bottom room." Roy ordered.

Jay and I set out to find the room on the blueprints, but there was no door in sight.

I shook my head, confused.

"The access point should be right here. I memorized those schematics, I know it." I muttered.

Roy walked up as soon as I finished speaking, and Scarlet arrived shortly after.

"What were you saying about the access point?" She asked.

I shook my head and pointed to the ground on the right.

"There should be an entrance right there. But there's no obvious point of entry." I said.

"Key word being: *obvious*." Jay replied, getting down on all fours.

He inspected the ground carefully, and after a moment, pointed to one of the tiles.

"Here. It's gotta be it. The rest of the floor is made of linoleum, but this one is a fake." He declared.

Roy walked up just as Jay stood, and Roy kneeled down by the tile.

"Here goes nothing." Roy muttered, and pressed down on the

tile with his gloved right hand.

It moved inward, and a shelf on the right wall jutted out and slid to the side, revealing a dimly lit staircase.

"Nice work." I told Jay, adjusting the strap on my quiver.

Jay smiled at my praise, his hazel eyes warm and glowing.

Roy stepped past us into the threshold of the door, and silently motioned for us to follow.

Scarlet elbowed me as we descended underground, and I was grateful for the lack of light, or else she would have seen me blush.

We finally arrived at a door, and Roy plucked a small camera and wire out from his utility belt.

He attached the two together, and snaked the device through the bottom of the door, pulling up visuals on his HoloWatch. From there, we could see Xavier Bêche, along with 13 other men and women, gathered around a table with papers in front of them.

"This is it," Roy whispered as low as he could, putting away the camera and cord.

"Ready," He started.

I unclipped by bow from my belt and unfolded it to its full size.

Scarlet pulled out a retractable staff from her boot, and Roy and Jay wielded Tranquilizer Guns (TG's).

We may have been spies, but O.U.O didn't supply underage youths with obviously lethal weapons.

Luckily, Roy wasn't underage, which is why he had his TG, and he lent his extra one to Jay.

"Set," Roy continued, pressing his back against the wall as we did the same.

I drew back an arrow, and Scarlet let her staff grow to its fullest length.

Jay had his eyes closed, as if silently hoping for something, and when he opened them again, a fire raged behind them before dying down to his normal gaze.

I looked over at Roy, determined to stay focused.

Roy crawled forward, and gave the knob a slow, unnoticeable turn... Locked.

He was going to have to barge right through.

He got into position, shoulder out, legs taut.

"Go!" He ordered, and charged at the door.

In one swift blow, the door was banged open, hung off one hinge, and slammed against the wall.

"O.U.O! Stop what you're doing, get to your feet, and put your hands up! I said, *HANDS UP!*" Roy bellowed.

8 out of the 14 people in the room did as they were told, while the others stayed in shock.

"Did I stutter? *GET UP!*" He exclaimed in French, pointing his TG at a group of people who stayed seated.

One by one, everyone in the room rose, including Xavier himself.

He was the only one without his hands in the air.

"Xavier Bêche, put your hands up. You, along with everyone else here, are under arrest for conspiracy charges." Roy told him in English. "*Mettez vos mains.*" Roy ordered, and still, Xavier didn't move.

"What is this? Coming into my meeting, accusing me and my colleagues of something this atrocious? It's repulsive! Who gave you the right…" Xavier trailed off when he spotted Jay, whose TG was aimed right at Xavier's chest.

Anger flared behind Xavier's brown eyes, and a strand of his black hair fell across his light skin as he growled, "You. You *rat! Traître!* How dare you take part in this, this, *betrayal!*"

Jay held his ground, unwavering.

"How dare you take part in this selfish, inhumane plan! Did you plan it all yourself? Or did you have help? The genius of the details far surpassed *your* level of craftsmanship…"

"You, little, *RAT! Traître!* That's what you are! What would your father think of you now?!" Xavier exploded at Jay's remark, and Roy stepped forward, his finger ready to squeeze the trigger.

"Put. Your hands. *UP!*" Roy ordered one last time.

Jay's expression changed from cold as ice to fiery as an inferno, and I knew it took all of his willpower not to fire at Xavier until every last bullet was gone.

My patience was starting to wear thin.

I took aim and shot an arrow at Xavier's right hand, hitting my mark.

The arrow missed his hand, as I had intended, but had struck a paper, dead center.

Xavier stayed staring at where the arrow stood, then glanced at his hand, in shock.

He looked at me, angrily, but I had already drew back another arrow that was aimed at his chest.

"Do as he says. You don't get a second warning." I ordered.

Xavier pressed his lips together, obviously in a tough spot.

A man tried to inch his way out the door and run, but Scarlet hit the ground hard where he stood with her staff, forcing them to keep their place.

A woman behind Xavier slowly lowered her hands, so slow you didn't notice the movement.

She had already gotten halfway into reaching into her coat pocket, and Roy exclaimed, "Hands up, I said! No movement!"

The woman froze, shocked at being caught.

In the span of one minute, chaos erupted.

The woman looked like she was going to put her hands up again, she even moved her hand away from her coat.

But in one fast move, she reached in a pressed a button, an obvious distress signal.

No sooner than a second after the button was pressed, Roy fired his TG, a small tranquilizer bullet flying out, and hitting the woman in the chest.

Her face grew drowsy and she fell to the floor, followed by silence in the room.

Suddenly, a door burst open from upstairs, and I knew we were about to receive some new guests.

"Company's coming!" I exclaimed, moving so that my back wasn't to the door.

No sooner had I said it, five armed men (obviously the woman's body guards) ran into the room, guns out of their holster, and ready to fire.

Scarlet hit the first man hard on the shin with her staff, and he stumbled before she kneed him in the chest and grabbed his weapon.

Jay shot two of the men with his TG, and they fell hard on the floor.

The men and women tried to escape the room through the door we had entered, and Roy and I fought them off pretty well.

Roy fired 5 times and hit 5 people, who lay passed out on the ground.

I fired arrows at four people, pinning their clothing to the walls and ground.

10 criminals down, four to go.

Roy turned his attention to the new wave of body guards that had entered the room, and he and Scarlet tried their best to fend them off.

After a moment, three gunshots were heard, fired one after another.

One ricocheted off of a metal filing cabinet and landed in the wall, while another pierced the ceiling.

One whizzed right by Xavier's ear, clearly too close for comfort.

"Shots fired, shots fired!" Roy shouted, kicking the table so that it fell over, acting like a shield.

Scarlet, Jay and I dove behind it to shield ourselves, and Roy fired at the man who had shot at him, causing him to pass out as well.

I watched as a man and woman tried to escape, only to be tripped by Scarlet's staff and shot by Jay.

I fired an arrow at one body guard's hand, knocking the weapon full force right out of his hands.

I did the same thing to one other body guard's gun, before Roy shot them both, and they fell to the ground, unconscious.

It was then that he caught my eye.

Xavier had made his over to the far left wall, and was frantically pushing different spots.

It took me a split second to process what was happening, but in a spy's life…

A split second could mean life or death.

A bullet smacked the table right by my ear, and I ducked further down behind it.

Xavier placed his hand over one promising spot and pushed, revealing yet another hidden passage none of us knew about.

Before anyone could stop me, I shouted, "Bêche is moving, pursuing target!"

I knelt down and took off running, determined to stop Xavier in his tracks.

"Runt!" I heard Roy yell, the shoot-like sounds of his TG following after.

I didn't turn back.

I knew he wasn't calling me; that's not what he was trying to do, no.

He was telling me to be careful.

I ran through the door and up the stairs, taking them two by two, not letting Xavier out of my sight.

He wouldn't get away.

That's not how the mission would end.

At least, that's what I thought.

Chapter Twenty Four

I fired arrows at Xavier's back, trying to pin him to a wall or get him to at least stop running.

Instead, he only sprinted faster, yelling curses in French as he broke through to the main floor.

He took off to the back emergency exit where I followed close behind.

I continued firing arrows, but my goal of not hitting him anywhere that would cause major problems prevented me from pinning him the way I wanted to.

Eventually, I gave up on that goal and fired an arrow right at his calf, which pierced his slacks and caused him to stop and howl in pain.

I stepped up to him and said, "It's over, Bêche. You're under-"
But I never finished.

Xavier pulled a gun out from his coat, one he had obviously snatched in his mad dash to escape.

One look at the gun and I dove behind a counter, his bullets hitting his own laptops and speakers instead of me.

I caught a glimpse of him in the refection of a flat screen TV, and I flinched as he pulled my arrow right out of his calf, firing the gun as a reflex from his pain.

I used that spare moment to rise, arrow drawn back, ready to fire.

A man came from the window we had entered, gun held up at me.

I ducked so low as a precaution so that if he fired, he would have missed me.

I shot an arrow at him before he could think, knocking his weapon out of his hands.

He didn't waste any time.

He grabbed Xavier and began dragging him towards the window, Xavier trying his best to limp behind.

I fired one more arrow at the man's jacket, pinning him to a wall.

That was arrow number 16, I only had four left.

I figured I was safe, an assumption I made too soon.

The man yelled and ripped his jacket from the wall, freeing himself.

In one quick movement, he had grabbed Xavier, pushed him through the window, and was following after him.

I quickly fired another arrow, narrowly missing his leg, and I climbed out after them.

A sharp gust of fierce, perpetual, wind hit me as soon as I got onto the roof, and the sight of whirling metal blades attached to Xavier's hope for escape greeted me.

His chopper was ready and waiting.

But so was I.

I fired an arrow at the pilot, who ducked and nonchalantly regained control of the helicopter.

Two arrows left.

I fired once more, hitting Xavier's daring escape partner smack in his brawny shoulder.

The man howled, and tried not to grip his shoulder in pain.

He had made it to the helicopter, and pushed Xavier in, flinging himself inside afterwards.

I had one shot.

My final arrow.

My last chance.

This arrow was no ordinary arrow, no.

It was a grappling hook.

I pulled it out of my quiver, quickly checking that it was ready and secure to fire.

I took stance, took aim, and had my mark in sight.

I drew back my bow just a bit further, wanting the impact to really stick.

My fingers were already moving, the arrow moving towards its target.

But it never hit its mark.

I was almost knocked off of my feet by two strong hands that held my bow, pushing it down towards the ground.

Instinct took over, and I used my adversary's own momentum to swing up, in an attempt turn the tables on them.

I looked up at my attacker's face, ready to knee them in the gut. Hard.

A familiar pair of deep, troubled hazel eyes made me stop in my tracks.

"Jay?" I asked, completely caught off guard.

"Delilah, STOP!" He yelled, attempting to keep my bow, and aim, down.

"What are you doing?! He's going to get away!" I shouted.

No sooner had the words left my mouth, the chopper became airborne, lifting away from the roof top and throwing painful stints of air at our faces.

I squinted against it, watching as the immense, black metal that held one of the most dangerous criminals on the planet began to shrink in the distance.

"NO!" I shouted, breaking free of Jay's hold.

I took aim at the helicopter once again, this time, without Jay trying to stop me.

"Don't waste your time. It's out of range." He said, out of breath.

I hated to admit it, but he was right.

If I took aim and fired then, I wouldn't have been able to stay hanging from the chopper the way I would have been before.

I whirled on Jay, anger boiling up underneath my skin, blood boiling in my veins.

"What were you thinking?! I had him! I was *so close!*" I

exclaimed, exasperated.

Jay looked at me with his deep gaze, hazel eyes glowing in the moonlight.

"Yeah, you were close. Close to nearly getting yourself killed. I was only trying to save you!" He shot back.

"Don't you get it? I don't need you to save me! I don't need your protection! All I hear from you is how I need to be careful, but you know what? It's my *job* to go out and *be* in danger! I can't help it! Will you *ever* understand that?!" I exclaimed, all of my frustration pouring out in a single rant.

Jay blinked, stunned that I had snapped at him like that.

He walked towards me, grabbed my bow, and let it fall to the ground.

He locked his immensely deep gaze on me, forcing me to stare back.

"Don't *you* get it? You have people that care about you more than you know. By throwing yourself in these kinds of situations, what do you think that does to the people who care? I've told you before, Delilah, there are bad people doing worse things in this world. You don't need to be out here, throwing yourself in their line of fire. One wrong move, and you're given a death sentence. One you may not even know about. But do you care? No, you go out saving the world, playing the hero. Good and bad isn't as black and white as everyone makes it out to be. The last thing I want is for you to get caught up in something bigger than you, and suffering because of it," he pressed his lips together before saying, "Trust me, I know how this side of the law works."

He took my hands in his, only adding to the effect of his pleas of wanting me to stay safe.

It was then that I looked at him, really looked him, for what he really was.

A scared boy who had found someone to care about, someone he could protect, someone who could give him purpose.

Someone who looked at him and didn't see a lowly thief, no, they saw what was behind those beautiful hazel eyes.

That someone… was me.

The anger slowly dispersed through my skin, as his words resonated in my head.

I took a deep breath, thinking of the right thing to say that could console him after his confession.

"I know you think that way. You think that because you know how these people think you can help keep me out of harm's way. But that sad truth is, you can't. People are going to get hurt, it will always happen. The real protection comes when you have someone to pick you back up, and fight for what you believe in, until there's no one left to fight. You can't keep everyone safe. You know that, don't you?" I asked, making him look me in my green gaze.

Jay stayed quiet for a moment, letting my words sink in.

He nodded, saying, "I know. But that doesn't mean I won't try. Remember…"

"The world is a dangerous place."

To Be Continued…

END

CPSIA information can be obtained
at www.ICGtesting.com
Printed in the USA
LVHW030711240222
711845LV00001B/1